A Susquehanna Tale

Robert John Andrews

CATAMOUNT
PRESS

an imprint of Sunbury Press, Inc.
Mechanicsburg, PA USA

CATAMOUNT
PRESS

an imprint of Sunbury Press, Inc.
Mechanicsburg, PA USA

For information about special discounts for bulk purchases, please contact Sunbury Press Orders Dept. at (855) 338-8359 or orders@sunburypress.com.

To request one of our authors for speaking engagements or book signings, please contact Sunbury Press Publicity Dept. at publicity@sunburypress.com.

FIRST CATAMOUNT PRESS EDITION: October 2024

Set in Adobe Garamond Pro | Interior design by Crystal Devine | Cover by Mac Andrews | Edited by Debra Reynolds.

Publisher's Cataloging-in-Publication Data
Names: Andrews, Robert John, author.
Title: A Susquehanna tale / Robert John Andrews.
Description: First trade paperback edition. | Mechanicsburg, PA : Catamount Press, 2024.
Summary: It was the time of rifle, tomahawk, and knife. It was the time of plough, axe, and endurance. It was the time of hope and loss. 1750 to 1800. Colonial Susquehanna Valley. The contested boundary between hungry settlers and Iroquois Confederacy. It was the time of frontier scout, Alexander Tennant, and pioneer settler, Colonel William Montgomery.
Identifiers: ISBN : 979-8-88819-239-9 (softcover).
Subjects: HISTORY / United States / Colonial Period (1600-1775)| HISTORY / United States / Revolutionary Period (1775-1800) | FICTION / Historical / Colonial America & Revolution.

Designed in the USA
0 1 1 2 3 5 8 13 21 34 55

For the Love of Books!

Front cover image is a crop of: Edmund Darch Lewis, *Edge of a Forest on the Susquehanna River (Early Morning)* (1866), oil on canvas, courtesy of the Woodmere Museum, Philadelphia, Pennsylvania.

Acknowledgments

Writers, akin to preachers, frequently must beg the indulgence of those good names they borrow for a good cause. My apologies are offered to the legacy of Gilbert Tennant, of the famous Tennant family, for giving a son to him and his first wife. I offer additional penance for having this fictional son stray from the family's deserved fame as leaders throughout the 18th century in revivalist Presbyterian preaching and theological education. There's always one member of the family who heeds the call of wanderlust.

Less liberty was taken with the famous Montgomery family so dear to the town of Danville, Pennsylvania. The information provided by William M. Baillie in his first-rate biography of William Montgomery, "Pennsylvania Patriot General William Montgomery," provided the facts about this family from which I was able to weave speculative narratives in the hopes of conveying an intimate portrait of their personalities. Alexander's friendly use of the title, 'Colonel Montgomery' isn't a demotion in rank so much as a mark of affection and respect. Only toward the end of this story does the Colonel get promoted to General, as he did in real life, to the special delight of his youngest daughter. Alas, were an epilogue added, I would note how Ballie's work relates how Margaret would happily marry four years after she is teased by her father's frontiersman friend, only to die two years into her marriage at the age of 22. We are all tapers too. Some burn quicker and brighter.

I pray my neighbors will receive this tale as my gift to this town and river valley that I have grown to love. And despite being a born Jersey boy, it is the place I call home, an affection especially nurtured because of the friends and parishioners I was privileged to serve at the Grove Presbyterian Church for just shy of three decades.

Dear readers: come and visit, as I did when gathering facts and insights for this novella, the various temples of history and learning that bless our region. A special thank-you goes to the volunteers and staff who serve our community by serving in these essential institutions, lest we forget:

The Montour County Historical Society

The General Montgomery House and Boyd House Museum, Danville

Thomas Beaver Library, Danville

Columbia County Historical and Genealogical Society, Bloomsburg

Northumberland County Historical Society, Sunbury, with its front yard model of Fort Augusta

A local temple (née mobile tabernacle) with two legs and a guitar is local historian, minstrel, naturalist, and teacher Van Wagner who helped inspire me to bring this tale to life. If you want to know about the river or eels or trees, talk to Van. He sings a song about them. Rocks too.

May this tale also pay tribute to all those tribes whose ghosts stroll amongst us still. My aim was for the readers (local and well beyond local) to be able to experience the history of this region and honor those who forged, for good and ill, what we have inherited.

I thank my readers for their critiques, comments, and edits. Despite being a preacher, I sometimes know when to listen. Thank you Merry Hackenberg, Francis Moyer, John and Spring Gardiner, Don Weber, Marty Walzer, historian Don King, Diana and Gary Boden, and my Danville News newspaper editor Eric Pehowic. Then there's my road-trip researcher and photographer, Frank Bastian, who patiently listened as I monologued my story ideas. The same goes to our two daughters, although they offered more direct advice as daughters will.

I'd be remiss if I failed to expression my gratitude to Sunbury Press for their professionalism, especially a patient editor named Debra Reynolds, and for taking a chance on a mere novella.

The best way to express appreciation to our son, Mac Andrews, already is in your hands with this chance for you to admire his artwork.

When it comes time for thanking my forbearing wife, Elaine, all I can say is that it has been quite a moondance. Waterford crystal glasses of prosecco clinking.

Last, I give thanks to the Susquehanna River herself, having traveled to both headwaters: the western headwaters near Carrolltown, and the north branch headwaters of Lake Otsego at Cooperstown.

A river never is the same river, yet the same. How old is Susquehanna? Likely as old as 324 million years, the end of the Permian and beginning of the Triassic age, a witness to Pangea, to the ice age, to one mass extinction when 96% of all species died and yet another extinction when 80% of all species died. Imagine all the comings and goings. The elvers turned eels, the shad runs, the cleansing mussels. The crops she nourished. The life she bequeathed. The blood her waters have washed away.

Our turn too. Throughout all our history, she has kept on flowing. She'll keep flowing long after my ashes are buried in my beloved Grove Presbyterian Church's memorial garden.

Surely the more tantalizing question might be not how old is she but how young is she?

Roll on.

Roll on, river.

Timeline

1711	Madam Montour moves into Otstonwakin (I use the spelling confirmed by a Montoursville historian, retired teacher, and elder in the Presbyterian church)
July 10, 1730	Birth of Alexander Tennant
August 3, 1736	Birth of William Montgomery
1738	Birth of Daniel Montgomery, brother
1742	Shikellamy arrives at Shamokin Village
1746	College of New Jersey founded in Elizabeth, New Jersey
1748	Tennant Leaves the College of New Jersey for the Frontier
	Death of Shikellamy
May 24, 1750	Burnt Cabins, Sidneysville
1754	French and Indian Wars begin
July 9, 1755	Braddock's defeat and retreat
October 16, 1755	Penn's Creek Massacre
1756	Morris declares war on Delawares, enacts scalping bounty
	Shamokin Village abandoned
	Fort Augusta built
	William Montgomery marries Margaret
1763	Conestoga massacre by Paxton Boys
	Pontiac Wars around Great Lakes

October 30, 1765	Birth of Daniel Montgomery, son
1772	William Montgomery marries Isabella
April 5, 1773	Birth of Robert Montgomery, son
April 1775–March 1776	Siege of Boston
Spring 1777	Montgomerys relocate to Montgomery's Landing, later renamed Danville
October 8, 1777	Birth of Alexander Montgomery, son
June 24, 1778	Solar Eclipse
July 1778	Big Runaway
July 3, 1778	Wyoming Massacre
July 29, 1779	Little Runaway and massacre of Fort Freeland
January 8, 1784	Birth of Margaret Montgomery, daughter
1793–1795	William Montgomery serves in the 3rd Congress in Philadelphia
1793	William Montgomery marries Hannah
1794	Priestly arrives in Northumberland
	Coleridge writes Pantisocracy poem, never published in his lifetime
1800	Alexander Tennant is 70 years old
	William Montgomery is 64 years old
	Son Daniel is shy of 35
	Son Alexander is shy of 23
	Daughter Margaret is 16 (dies at 22)

1806	Daughter Margaret dies two years after her marriage
1816	Death of William Montgomery
1831	Death of Daniel Montgomery, son
1848	Death of Alexander Montgomery, son

Place Names

Onayutta . . . Juniata

Lawi-saquick . . . Loyalsock

Legauihanne . . . Lycoming

Mechek-menatey . . . Great Island

Kaarondinhah . . . Penns Creek

Popemetang . . . Roaring Creek

Ohi-yo . . . Ohio

Alleghane . . . Alleghany

Nit-a-nees . . . Nittany

Achsinnimahoni / . . . Sinnemahoning
Sinnemahoning

Konondaigua . . . Canandaigua

Chesepiooc . . . Chesapeake

Menaonkihela . . . Monongahela

Patowmac . . . Potomac

Kithanink . . . Kittanning

Sheshequanink . . . Sheshequin Path

Chililsaugi . . . Chillisquaque

Catawese . . . Catawissa

Mahonhanne . . . Mahoning

Azilum . . . Located in Bradford
County, Pa.

Ischue . . . Olean Creek

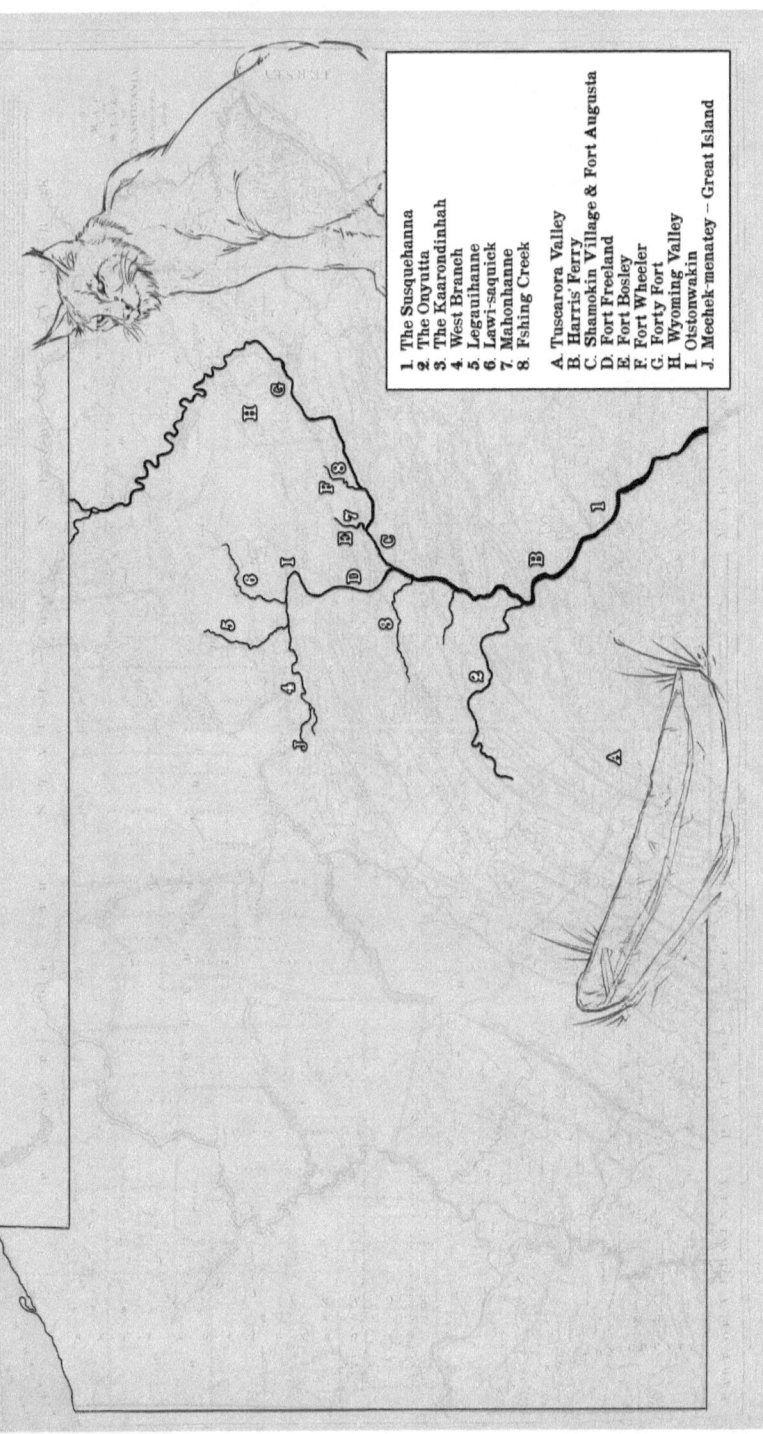

1. The Susquehanna
2. The Onyutta
3. The Kaarondinhah
4. West Branch
5. Legauihanne
6. Lawi-saquick
7. Mahonhanne
8. Fshing Creek

A. Tuscarora Valley
B. Harris's Ferry
C. Shamokin Village & Fort Augusta
D. Fort Freeland
E. Fort Bosley
F. Fort Wheeler
G. Forty Fort
H. Wyoming Valley
I. Otstonwakin
J. Mechek menatey – Great Island

CHAPTER ONE

1800

"William," the voice called down the hallway from the attached kitchen. "William! Would you find a moment to come here, please?"

"Mistress Hannah summons. Something must be amiss. Excuse me. I'll be right back," apologized Colonel William Montgomery.

The visitor rose from the padded bench and walked over toward the window to the left of the fireplace. Ruth waggled behind him and rested her white snout on her paws, her liver-colored ears drooped. With his back to the entrance to the room, the visitor gave no notice of seeing the young woman peering around the door jamb. She was no longer child nor girl, yet innocent enough to still giggle when she saw visiting her father a man, unlike most men she'd seen, fully bearded, wearing black boots, brown breeches, a linen hunting shirt, no waistcoat, and a green hunting frock. His black and white patterned neckerchief was tied loosely around his neck.

She watched him as he looked out through the parlor window across the field toward the sawmill and gristmill, both constructed, similar to the Colonel's house, of fieldstone. A small collection of books lay stacked on the top of a table beneath the window and had raised his curiosity from the moment he was led into the sitting room by the Colonel. It had been several months since he had opened a book. On top were several copies of old almanacs. One book was a collection of Psalms. Leaning against the small pile was a large, illustrated edition of *The Pilgrim's Progress*.

Another book was a copy of Adam Smith's *The Theory of Moral Sentiments*. On the bottom of the pile was *Poems on Several Occasions* by John Donne. He pulled it out and opened the cover to reveal the tan marbled goatskin end-paper. He read, published in London by J. Tonson, 1719. He caressed the smooth, burgundy-colored spine with his gnarled hand. Tennent began to thumb through the pages, looking for favorites from his earlier life. Several of the pages remained uncut. He looked around for a paper knife. Seeing none handy, he reached into his right boot and pulled out a small knife, with which he slit open the pages at the bottom fold. Blinking and holding the book at a distance, he found the poem for which he was searching. In a low voice he intoned a few lines:

> "Call us what you will,
> wee are made such by love;
> call her one, mee another flye,
> We're all Tapers too,
> and at our own cost die . . ."

A giggle interrupted his reading. Without turning his eyes away from the book, the visitor said with a playful lilt in his voice, "Such are the fortunes of an aged and hoary hunter. I can barely hear the scamper of a mouse across the floor, but I can still hear a giggle. My eyes might no longer be capable of counting the eyelashes of a doe in the woods, but I can still see the color of a young girl's eyes." He turned and bowed to the young woman. She wore the customary white linen cap, a light blue, elbow-length bodice match-ing her dark blue wrap-around petticoat, leather buckled shoes, and white apron, with a rose-colored scarf draped over her shoulders.

"Would you then be Margaret?'

She curtsied in reply. "I am, sir." She turned aside and blushed. "Please forgive me for giggling, sir. I meant no disrespect."

"None at all taken, lass. If I were to look at me, I'd giggle too. He grinned broadly. "As a matter of fact, Margaret Montgomery, when I am spotted in the woods dressed like this, crows laugh at me, magpies screech, frogs prance on hind legs they are so amused. Even squirrels chatter amongst themselves, thinking me odd, mocking me despite me carrying my rifle in the hollow of my arm and hungry for squirrel pie. Do I frighten them? I frighten them not a wink."

"My father speaks of you, Mr. Tennent, often, though I could barely credit what he said. I thought him teasing me with another of his fictions. Father does like to tease in his gentle natured way." Ruth approached the young woman to sniff her feet and apron. Margaret reached down and petted her neck. Ruth licked her hand and rested against her feet.

"Well, young Margaret, I wouldn't mind being one of your father's fictions if it makes a young woman laugh. A young woman's laughter is the sweetest sound there is. Although we have met before, when you were a mere child and had far better distractions." Tennent looked down at Ruth. "I also judge Ruth a good judge of character. 'Tis pleasant at my age to have a dog these days. Never could before. They had a habit of getting too excited in the hunt. But yes, your father and I have shared a few adventures together. All remain as memories, and I'm rather uncertain how many more I will create, now that my hair pulled back is as gray as the hair on my face. We who have lived more often in the wilderness than towns find that we blend in better with the other critters of the forest. We tend to shave only in town when there is a fair chance to be shaven by a razor that is more sharp than rusty."

"I do hope you will yet create as many memories as you can imagine."

"You are kind. Although, young lady, there is a hazard with being so shaggy. Once upon a time I had a friend, who was out on a hunt for bear with his best friend. His friend was far shaggier than I am now. They spread out to hunt separately. The friend spotted a furry black bear, took aim, and killed it straightaway. One shot. It was only after he gutted the bear and began to skin it that he realized it was his best friend."

"I don't believe you, Mr. Tennent." She beamed bright enough to fill the room with sunshine. She pointed at the book in his hands. "I like what you were reading. It sounded sad yet beautiful."

"Poets are like that, especially Doctor Donne. At least before he became Dean of St. Paul's and wrote his religious sonnets. You should read it." Tennent raised his fingers to his lips, whispering, inviting her playfully into the secret, "I do believe Mr. Tonson edited out of this publication Donne's more scandalous poems, more's the pity."

"Most of my reading tends to be of a practical nature," she pouted. "Recipes and formulas for making medicinals, which our grandmothers and aunts have written down for when we are married. How to prepare Scotch Eggs or Pop

Robbins. How to make plasters for the chest, ointments for hives, or a recipe for dysentery." Margaret's face turned prim as she folded her hands upon her apron. "Two tea-spoonsful of charcoal, one tablespoonful of Old Jamaican Spirits, one of molasses, two of sweet oils—dosage one-half tablespoonful every two or three hours."

"A fine recitation, Miss Montgomery. My compli-ments. Quite necessary lessons too, at times. Ah, lass, when one reads a poem, however, you enter a different kind of world, that takes our world of dysentery and plasters, hives and Pop Robbins, our world of lovely young women and doddering old men, and gives them meaning. If the writer be both sad and beautiful rather than merely sentimental, it can be as mysterious and enchanting a world as entering a new forest where no one has set footprints before."

"You sound like a poet yourself."

"No, pet, I cannot create so much as observe," he replied with a wink.

"Father said once, I remember, how it was a poet that brought you together, that time when you saved his life."

"Your father is a great and good man, but he gives me far more credit than is deserving."

"Tell me, please."

"I demur. You should ask him again. It is his story to tell."

"No, please. I've heard his version. I'd like to hear yours. Father often exaggerates."

CHAPTER TWO

1800

"There's really little to tell," Tennent stalled.

Margaret, imbued with a charm that could blend modesty with insistence, was not so easily dismissed.

"Well, come inside here and let's sit down." Ruth resumed her position to the left of the bench. The Bracket clock on the mantel began chiming. "Eleven o'clock already? I must be brief, dear Margaret." He inhaled a deep breath. "It was during the early days of the Revolution when we Continentals laid siege to Boston. A group of us who were known to have a particular felicity in arms had been recruited to pester the British. I had occasion to work for General Washington years earlier, when he was a frustrated colonial Captain serving under General Braddock."

Colonel Montgomery had entered the room unnoticed except by Ruth. He coughed. "You 'had an occasion to work for the good General?'" he repeated, enjoying teasing Tennent. "More like one of Washington's top scouts."

Tennent and daughter turned to look up at him. Tennent reached down to scratch Ruth behind the ear.

"Now, Margaret," said the Colonel, "please go help your mother prepare dinner. Your uncle's daughters are busily twirling the chicken. Your mother frets that your naughty namesake and Isabella are playing much too much with the string, rather than paying attention to roasting our meal. They need their older cousin to attend and keep them mindful. Besides," the Colonel's voice twinkled, "you shouldn't stay much longer because, well, didn't you realize that I've asked Mr. Tennent here to discuss your dowry?"

Margaret's cheeks and throat blushed deep red as she tsked, "Oh father!" Tennent rubbed his forehead, then held up his hands to her to protest his innocence.

Montgomery continued, "Alright then. Stay for a moment, my dear. Your mother can wait. I've told the full story to your brothers. I suppose you should hear it too." He scratched his chin. "Margaret," he said, lowering his voice, "you ought to know that my reputation isn't exactly what many think it is. My brother John in North Carolina is the true military man of the family—wounded, captured by Cornwallis, and yet the man still escaped to fight another day."

"Father, you're treated as a hero. They've made you a General."

"Of the local militia, my dear. Purely honorific and ceremonial. I do believe it's only because I look rather splendid on horseback in my uniform." He looked over at Tennent and grinned. "The way true soldiers should look—shiny buttons, fancy lace epaulettes, and their stockings clean and white."

"You do, father, you do look splendid in your uniform, very gallant."

"Yes, well, the posting for the Seventh Division of Militia is up for renewal this year—not that I've earned it. We shall see what the martial god of war decrees."

Offering a lazy military salute followed by a playful tug of the forelock, Tennent teased, "I suppose I should refer to you as General then, not Colonel."

"Don't you dare, old scout. Yes, Margaret, as the story goes, back in the early days of the Revolution I commanded two regiments. Truth be told, my role was only on paper. I marched only on paper. The men who served in those battalions did brave service, nothing paper about them. Grand fellows all. Remember also, Margaret, enlistments in those early days of the war were for two months. We were militia. We were farmers. We had farms to work and families to raise. Plowing, harvesting, tending to the livestock, milking, tilling. Not all men had sons. These farmers were willing to spend a month or two in defense of their homeland. Understand, they weren't regular soldiers, however. We were militia. Yes, in name I commanded two battalions, or regiments if you prefer. The Associators and the Flying Camp, both from Chester County."

Margaret listened attentively, trying to imagine those days.

Montgomery pursed his lips. "I never commanded in the field. Better men did that, men named Bull, Evans, McDowell. While they fought and suffered in Long Island, at the garrison of Fort Washington near the Harlem River, then in Trenton and Princetown, I carried out my duties back home in politics and supplies."

Tennent chimed in, "We all serve. If there are no supplies, no organization, no recruitment, there is no army. It's tooth to tail. Some men are the teeth, some men feed the teeth so it can bite."

"Understand, dear, we were forming a nation and a commonwealth. My responsibility was to make sure my troops had the gunpowder and food they needed. Our task, in the various Congresses that met, was to give them means to fight for independence. When you require men to kill or be killed, you need to give them a reason, a cause. Dignity. Ours was the dignity of defending our homes, our land, our rights, securing our freedom from British tyranny. Our Father in Heaven, who abhors the aggressor, will stand beside those who suffer the aggressor's arrogance, those who wish never to fight but who believe they have been given no other option."

The Colonel breathed a cleansing breath and relaxed back into his chair. "I'm rehearsing my speech again." He looked over at his patient daughter. "It also became obvious by winter of 1777 that militias had their place, but wars needed to be fought by trained and disciplined regular armies. Discipline is the surest tonic for fear. My Flying Camp did good service at the Battle of Princetown, first as a decoy outside Trenton, then when some companies were thrown into the fray at Princetown. Mr. Tennent was there, weren't you?"

Tennent nodded in assent.

Margaret, aglow, asked, "You served General Washington again?"

Montgomery continued, gesturing toward Tennent. "I remember you telling me on another occasion how our good General captured an entire wagon train of British supplies. But Margaret, listen now and promise me, this information must remain a military secret, because Washington, frustrated by the debates in Philadelphia, failed to inform the Continental Congress of this fact, assuming the Congress would accordingly reduce the supplies they were obliged to send the army."

Margaret placed her hand over her mouth and feigned shock. Then she crossed her heart.

With a mischievous mien, Tennent looked over at Margaret and again raised his right hand. "On my honor, I can neither dispute nor testify to this deceit by our then-future President." He lowered his hand to his lap and raised his eyes to the ceiling. "Those were lean and trying times."

"Still," the Colonel pressed on. "All these failures among others exposed too clearly the weakness and inconstancy of our militia. I read the reports. General Mercer commanded the militias who fought bravely against the British, but British musketry proved faster than the fire of our rifles. We were deadlier but they were faster. Then Mercer, who didn't understand militia at all, called for a bayonet charge. He paid the ultimate price for his ignorance. Militias use hunting rifles; we didn't carry bayonets. It was a disaster, a rout. At least until the General himself rode forth, rallied the men, and together militia and regulars found their mettle, held their ground, advanced, and won the day. How he wasn't wounded, I cannot imagine. Surely God's hand protected him."

"Colonel," Tennent interrupted. "You're speechifying."

"An elder statesman's prerogative," Montgomery replied in a half-hearted apology. You forget, I'm preparing my speech for July 4th."

Tennent pointed toward the fireplace. "I notice the absence of a bellows."

The Colonel shrugged. "You never need one when a politician is in the room."

"Or a preacher," grinned Tennent, remembering fondly his long dead father and uncles.

"Father," Margaret reminded them, "what about Boston?"

"Yes, dear. Thank you. Boston was the only time I commanded in the field. It was a siege rather than a battle.

My battalion was called up to provide relief, reinforcement. We spent our time, like farmers, digging entrenchments, felling trees, fortifying breastworks, taking turns at guard duty, filling gabions. Important work, although very little true soldiering."

"Yet," corrected Tennent, "that, too, is soldiering."

"Not your kind, old friend. We did what we could, but the occasional British sorties were repulsed by the trained soldiers. Or, Margaret, by men such as this man in this room now. The good General appreciated their talents with the rifle. Their rifles kept the British lobster-backs honest. They kept them pinned down, at least until Knox hauled Ticonderoga's cannon to bear down on them and forced the King's men to set sail and evacuate to New York."

"Margaret," Tennent added with a timbre of confession in his voice, "we did more than pester them. It was a disagreeable business, but war is a disagreeable business. We scouts were tasked with killing as many officers as we could."

Margaret looked down and smoothed her apron across her lap.

Montgomery continued, "One chilly afternoon, I had taken a company of men to strengthen a redoubt, when, after the crack of a rifle near me, I hear this kneeling, leather-stocking scout quote Cicero. I stood beside him, looked down at him, and laughed, telling him I've never before met a humble frontiersman who could quote Cicero."

"You, Mr. Tennent?"

"Me? Yes. I should excuse myself by explaining that I come from a family of scholars. Professors and preachers. All save one."

"Every time this man's aim was deadly accurate, this leather-stocking from the woods would mutter that famous line from Cicero's Philippic, in Latin no less: *O fortunate mors quae naturae debita pro patria est potisimum reddita.*"

"Now Father, there's little Latin here in Montgomery's Settlement, especially for us young women. All we get for school lessons from Mistress Jane are New England Primers. 'In Adam's fall, we sinned all. A dog will bite a thief at night.'" Margaret reached out toward Tennent's hand. "Do tell, what does the quotation mean?"

"An unfortunate amusement on my part," apologized Tennent. "It means 'O fortunate death which, due to nature, is most preferably paid for one's native country.'" Tennent muttered softly, "I was a younger man back then. Young men can be raw and prideful."

"Is that when you saved father's life?"

"A matter of fortune, chance, or providence. Perhaps luck. While reloading my rifle and searching for a new target, I noticed a puff from one of the British frigate's cannons. Somehow those clever tars figured out a way to elevate the barrel."

"Suddenly," Montgomery intruded to finish the narrative, "this man leapt at me, threw me to the ground, and covered me with his own body, just as the exploding cannon shell struck the front of the redoubt, showering us in dirt and branches. A near miss for both of us, certain disaster for me if I had remained standing like the scarecrow fool I was."

Silence pervaded the room for a minute, the only sound coming from the gears of the Bracket clock.

Colonel Montgomery, lost in his memories, finally reached for his daughter's hand and patted it, saying,

"Enough tales for you, young lady. Off you go to help your mother. You may tell her I got caught up telling a story. She might forgive you then."

Daughter prepared to leave. Ruth wagged her tail in expectation of a scratch behind the ear. Margaret obliged. Ruth leaned into her fingers as she stood up and turned toward Tennent, folding her hands in front of her. "Thank you for being my father's friend; and thank you for talking to me about poetry." Turning aside, she repeated quietly, "We're all Tapers too . . ."

He again winked at her.

CHAPTER THREE

1800

"Fine young woman," Tennant said, after his friend's daughter padded down the planked floorboards of the hallway toward the kitchen and her younger cousins.

"A credit, a credit, she is. Brightest of the litter too. She looks fully her sixteen years, but her mind is far more mature, blessed with a merry and winsome wit. What Master Shakespeare would say, 'Faith, lady, she has a merry heart, it keeps on the windy side of care.' I have such hopes for her." The Colonel slapped his thigh. "And if you won't take her in marriage, I'll have to be on the lookout for another suitable suitor, I suppose."

"Yes, do suppose. A son-in-law ought never be older than the bride's father. Fortunate lad, indeed, whomever he be."

They sipped together and smiled together, the warmth of the rye reminding them of days of comfort earned from days of discomfort. The dog, resting to the left of the bench, closed her eyes in equal contentment. Montgomery stirred.

"The secret, old friend, is to distill the rye twice." From the decanter, Montgomery poured several ounces to refresh his visitor's glass. "Good health to you, Tennent, and do enjoy our late President's own recipe. We sip to their memories and to our past."

The welcomed visitor leaned forward from the padded bench and rolled the glass between his rough palms. "Well, Colonel, if you don't mind, I'd rather raise a glass to the future. Can't do much about the past, as you and I both know too well. Our gray heads prove that, but as you've shown with what you and your family have done here, there's much we can do about what we hope to become."

"I thank you for that, Tennent. Right you are. As usual. Each of my sixty-four years thanks you for that sober reminder," said the gentleman courteously as he placed the decanter on the black stained lowboy. On top of a table was a candlestick draped in tallow. The old scout looked at the table with its three drawers and intricately carved cabriole legs, admiring the luxury of it and the rest of the room. The host tugged on the bottom edge of his ruby red waistcoat. "More than right, friend. By Jove, I've missed your candor. I suffer from that vaunted age when people are much too wary to disagree with me; or are much too full of pity that they cannot help but humor me. So," he said, raising his glass, "a toast to providence, industry, and hope. May our meager labors be judged worthy by those who succeed us."

Tennent carefully set his glass beside him on the bench and rubbed his finger around its rim. He laughed silently, as was his custom. He looked over at his host, who had settled down in the chair beside the fireplace. "Can't remember when I last drank from a real glass. Tankards, yes. Tin cup, yes. Gourds of water for most of my roving life. Glass makes the whiskey taste better somehow." He again chuckled silently. "Can't remember, either, when I last tasted fine rye."

"You could settle down, you've earned it. There's a place for you here always. You marked this region long before I did."

"Foxes have holes, and the birds of the air have nests; but the Son of man hath not where to lay his head."

"There you go, quoting the Bible at me. Now, now, old friend, our hard-fought peace has earned us a chance for a prosperous rest, to start reaping in earnest what we imagined and longed for those years ago. My son, Daniel, is busy working with his Uncle Daniel. When I relocated here, my brother Daniel risked all to follow me, you might remember, bringing his family here from the luxuries of Philadelphia. Used to finer things, he sacrificed a coddled life to build a new life here. Young Daniel has busied himself these months surveying and platting what promises to be a fine town, marking out lots to sell. I'm the farmer. Those two Daniels, by developing trade, are the ones really creating this town, this community. After all, surveying is in the family blood. My surveying work, I'm pleased to say, was crucial for the development of this entire northeast, along this North Branch to Wyoming Valley."

With a wry smile, Tennent shook his head, declining the Colonel's kind invitation to settle down. He drained his glass. "Maybe, Colonel, I'll become one of your townsfolk, but I doubt it. Water flows where it must," he continued. "I do appreciate your invitation. Seems as if your fine mansion has become the closest I have to a fixed home. Still, I desire to boat down the Ohi-yo someday and see that mother of all rivers they tell it flows into. Me and Ruth," he said, as he reached down behind her ear. Ruth, a mixed breed, although heavy on spaniel, leaned into it. "Then there are those stretches out west they call prairies. As much as I love my trees, I cannot imagine a landscape all grassland, barren of any canopy to shade the growth. Horizons, friend, have a pull I haven't yet escaped." Tennent lifted his right foot and wiggled it. "Besides, I'm not ready for the eternity box. This recent pair of boots hasn't worn out yet, like my moccasins do."

"You always are welcome here," the Colonel rejoined graciously. "Daniel plans to stop by to greet you, along with my youngest son, Alexander. Both are successful men, Daniel now with a family of his own. My Alexander—well, it seems that he's not too far behind his brother in Cupid's court. I think you'll find a kindred spirit in my Alexander." The Colonel paused. "I've always wondered, why don't you ever use your given name? Alexander is a fine name."

Tennent reached for Ruth again. "That school boy just faded away when I left New Jersey. Perhaps my first name carried with it too large a burden."

"We all fade away, I daresay. Me? I pray I'll be buried within view of my beloved Church. 'Tis a pretty grove up the lane supplied by a fresh spring. By the goodness of Divine Providence." The Colonel abruptly stood up, prompting Ruth to raise her head. "May I charge your glass again?" He did so before Tennent could reply. "It's the good General's own recipe. I prized it from Madison when I served in Congress a few years ago, where we became friends—stalwart Democratic Republicans fighting the good fight against those Federalists like Adams."

"All that aside, you, Colonel, did your country credit by passing the Slave Trade Act. I read about it months later when I was translating for Pickering and assisting with negotiations on what they finally called the Treaty of Konondaigua. Although, it took almost the same amount of time for them to agree what to name the treaty." Tennent laughed softly. "Beautiful lakes up north there. New York is filling up around those lakes. The handprint of God's blessings, they say. Amazing—almost four years now and that blessed treaty still holds. Cornplanter himself was among the fifty chiefs who signed it. If the Iroquois Confederacy could agree, perhaps even you fellows in Congress could also agree on something."

"Proud of that vote, yes indeed. Except for how we view this curse of slavery, I've always felt that I did have more in common with the Southern farmers than with the New England Yankees." The Colonel swirled the rye in his glass. "Tasty, isn't it? Seems Madison back in Virginia became acquainted with the fellow who became Washington's farm manager. Another good Scotsman. Where would our nation be without us Scot Presbyterians, eh?"

"*Slàinte mhath*," agreed Tennent, raising his glass in a toast.

"Good health to you too. And as you should readily admit, Tennent, Scots and whiskey have been known to carry on with some familiarity. We've borrowed the recipe: sixty percent rye, thirty-five percent corn, and five percent malted barley. All grown here. From our own fields and our neighbors' fields. One hundred eighty acres. Wheat plus buckwheat.

"Despite the shale, this is fertile ground, blessed by this protected valley, cool breezes from the west, and plentiful water. I knew there was opportunity here, from the first time I heard about this region, troubles aside. Water, water, water. Water for power. Water for crops. Water for livestock. You, man, need to keep a weather eye out for good land to purchase.

"All this comes from my own gristmill over on the Mahoning near the saw mill. Out here on the frontier, we farmers have to be self-sufficient. You can see the gristmill from this window. That's why I came here. It takes more than a strong back. Takes a strong will and stronger mind. How best to employ Gods' gifts. We are men of the Enlightenment; thanks be to God. Just consider our modern array of recent scientific advancements. I hold my Bible closest to my heart, but my almanac comes second."

The Colonel's penchant to turn a conversation into a speech always amused patient Tennent. No wonder, he chuckled privately into his glass of rye, the Colonel's been tasked to serve in a variety of important public positions. Church ruling elder, Judge, Colonel of Militia, State Assemblyman during the Revolution, Censor, State Senator, Congressional Representative. Despite Tennent being older by six years, the Colonel reminded Tennent of his father, especially when his father was standing beneath the sounding board in his Philadelphia pulpit, full of wise saws and sayings. When you got the gift . . . well, each to his own gift.

"We had the copper kettles brought in all the way from Philadelphia through Reading and the Centre Turnpike. Transportation, that's the key. Transportation. We rely on good roads. This river is a precious and providential gift," he said, looking southward through the front window of the sitting room, "but given its rocks and windings and its interminable islands, it is most unreliable for commerce all year long. Sleds are useful come an icy winter. Come springtime, yes, we can raft out our produce for trade or travel by Durham boats. The good General used Durham boats to cross the Delaware to attack Trenton."

"I remember quite well. It was damned cold."

The Colonel, animated by his own voice, continued. "Sometimes those bizarre arks float down from the new

French settlement, Azilum. But that was before that fellow Napoleon took over France last year and let the exiles return. We'd gather at the top of the crest when they drift by, the pole-men straining to avoid the rocks. There still are some folks who have expressed great hopes that trade can navigate this river from Baltimore to possibly the Great Lakes. What was it that Pascal wrote? Oh yes, that 'rivers are roads that move.' But the winding Susquehanna can be treacherous. Brother Daniel lost an entire shipment of grain plus two good men when they struck a rock just above Harris' Ferry. Set us back a bit. Pardon me, it's now called Harrisburg. Of course, four years ago come this October, the most popular water craft were pumpkins."

Tennent screwed up his face. "Pardon?"

"The Great Pumpkin Flood, they called it. Pumpkins floating everywhere for a week. We've gotten familiar with the Susquehanna flooding every four years or so. That particular flood washed out many a farmer's field and swept away all their harvest. No pumpkin pies for a year. Still, there is a reward. Rich loam. Daniel's trading post is located on the rise just before the banks of the river. Convenient access. Water promises trade."

"Colonel, you might do well to remember about this river is that where I haven't floated, either downriver or upriver, I've walked along all of its banks, from source to Chesapeake, West Branch too." Tennent teased, "You, Colonel Montgomery, ventured here after others blazed the trail, moving here after we met in Boston. What was that? Yes, 1777. Right? How fast it goes. There was no rye to share and sip from your excellent distillery. But then, our Commander kept me too busy to find time to share a jug of anything potent. When I explored here, twenty-five years before you built your log cabin on your hundred eighty acres, there were only mussel middens left behind by the Leni Lenape."

The Colonel barely paused, his sail hoisted and running with the wind. "Right you are, right you are. But roads, that's what we lack and that's what we are constructing now. Connecting all these settlements. Derrstown. Washingtonville. South of Williamsport where the battle of Muncy Hills was fought near the Warrior's Spring. Shamokin, now called Sunbury for Sunbury-on-Thames. Upstream settlements too. Clearing the way for post roads. It's astounding to imagine how a letter or newspaper from Philadelphia's Gazette, or the Oracle from Harris's Ferry, can arrive at the new post office in Northumberland, often within a week, weather depending. Five years ago, in 1795, that remarkable feat was impossible." Montgomery rubbed his chin. "Newspapers, huh . . ." he muttered. "Now that I hear myself talking about it, newspapers are like roads. Roads of communication. I'm convinced that if it weren't for newspapers there would be no United States of America. Vital was this wide and free exchange of ideas, information, arguments. Who was it who railed against 'offering up human sacrifices to the pride of tyrants.'"

"Paine, if I recall." Wanting to change the subject, Tennent observed, "I noticed the crews clearing those roads. I ran into several teams on my journey here. A far cry from my first venture into this region. Wagons can now traverse the paths."

"Look at what we have become. In less than two decades. Peace does give prosperity a chance, friend. You've seen what this has become. You won't find a stump between here and the Mahoning. I hope you'll visit Daniel's trading post. There's even a ferry. Sixteen years ago, there were only six small cabins. Sunbury now publishes their own paper, *The Sunbury and Northumberland Gazette*. In the last several years we've added a blacksmith, tinsmith, gunsmith, miller, painter, cooper, a physician even, to our settlement. We're thriving here. Given the red hue in the ore in these surrounding hills, I predict some grand opportunity will yet be revealed. Even our Presbyterian Church prospers, the gospel advancing in leaps and bounds to the glory of the Lord. We've had our own pastor for a year now, though shared with the Derry Church. The Reverend John Boyd Patterson. He lodged with us when he first came here. He'll regret missing you, especially when I explained you are the son of Gilbert Tennent. We began worship in my barn, now we have our own meeting house as well as a school. Some of us are thinking of subscriptions to establish an Academy."

"You may have noted that although the Bible begins in a garden, it concludes with a city."

"So it does, so it does," observed the Colonel, enjoying an audience this attentive and ready to banter. "It is about community. And now the Governor is appointing a commission to direct the digging of canals to connect us faster and easier."

An animated Colonel waved his hands expansively. "Soon we will produce apple brandy. It's a new era, already rich with marvelous possibilities, the cusp of a new century. Already planted one orchard east of here. Our neighbors are doing the same. We'll soon harvest apples from another orchard we planted in the field near where Daniel has mapped out Ferry Street. Newton Pippins. I'm planning on building an adjacent cider press. Listen to this, we're going to build it in the shape of an octagon so the horses can circle indoors in all weathers. In a couple of years, I'm planning on a woolen mill. You may have noticed I've begun breeding sheep." The Colonel raised a clenched fist and shook it. "Now, if only a certain one of my neighbors would control his unchaperoned rams better and keep them from turning feral and roaming after my ewes."

"If yet I have not all thy love, Deare, I shall never have it all . . ."

"None of your blasted poetry now, if you please, especially when I'm working myself up into a decent and proper pique. Besides, you're my audience, helping me rehearse for my address that I've been invited to deliver."

Tennent smiled at his friend's sanguine enthusiasm and proud ambitions. Yet behind his tender smile was tucked away a deeper sigh. He accepted long ago it would inevitably come to this. His work was part of what made this happen. His Lancaster rifle and tomahawk helped achieve the ascendency of axe and plow. Forests into farmland. Roads demanding hewn trees. Humanity was inevitable, and with humanity, imbalance. His decades of wanderings and conflict taught him far more than all his years of formal schooling, how nature seeks balance, how humankind disrupts. Is this—he mused, remembering how his father expected him to follow Tennent family tradition and enter into the Presbyterian ministry—what the Bible meant when Moses recorded God's words about dominion over all creation?

The way he felt and talked about the forests is how Colonel Montgomery felt and talked about towns.

The Colonel picked up the decanter and refreshed his glass and Tennent's. "Say, what was this talk of poetry, o' Cicero of the Wilderness?"

"From your *Donne's Poems on Several Occasions*. It's right over there. You do realize, Colonel, books are meant to be read, rather than merely decorative. I had to cut apart the pages."

"Books, yes. Poetry? I daresay books of poetry lack, for me, a necessary practicality. Which, I hasten to add, brings me to mention a recent conversation fresh from Doctor Priestly himself in Northumberland. You'll raise an eyebrow over this tale."

Tennent leaned back on the bench.

"At a recent commission meeting held at his house, the Doctor spoke to me, whence I detected a tone of disappointment. I pursued the matter. He had heard that a surge of enlightened young people in England had communicated with him and expressed their eagerness to join him here along the banks of the Susquehanna. The news buoyed Priestly's hopes for the region. He's been feeling adrift and abandoned lately and had hoped for fresh company from England. I daresay he's had enough of farmers and merchants."

Tennent grinned.

"Apparently, these young people were inspired by some of your presumably profound and starry-eyed poets, who envisioned arriving to our frontier and creating a romantical utopia, a oneness with nature to cultivate the sublime, cossetted refinement of human nature. Coleridge and Southey were two of the poets mentioned by Priestly. They had begun calling their fantasy 'Pantisocracy,' or some such puffery."

Tennent rubbed his temples and exhaled deeply.

"Well, Doctor Priestly confided to me how disappointed he was when he finally received word that a few souls did arrive on the shores of America, though upon arriving most took the next ship home. Coleridge and Southy never got the chance to set sail to America. They had planned to marry some sisters and create this Susquehanna community of natural bliss. But they called it off. Evidently their plans also were interrupted by some miffed pride about who was going to marry which sister."

The Colonel leaned back and laughed. "Human nature rarely surprises us Presbyterians. Their hopes and dreams were dismasted, not in the least when it finally dawned on them the amount of physical labor required for a self-sufficient utopia, such as felling their own trees and plowing their own fields."

"Odd. And quite the anecdote, Colonel, though I confess I refuse to be churlish or querulous these days," said Tennent. "Part of me feels sorry for them. Can we judge them for having a dream? We're all looking for something better."

"Such is the disturbing reality of reality, old friend; not to mention that these poets finally came to the realization that they were planning to relocate to and inhabit a country frequented by troublesome Iroquois, Delaware, Susquehannocks, Tuscarora, and, far worse, an over-abundance of pesky Scotsmen."

"That surely is enough to discourage the noblest idealists."

The Colonel again laughed roundly and finished his glass. "Aye, friend. Your chosen path has taken you to see aspects of life, both terrible and wonderful, that I never have nor will. I'm a farmer, a planter. Mayhap that's why we are friends. Perhaps a little envious of each other?"

"Pantisocracy, eh? Even I, fifty years ago, wasn't as naive as those romantics."

CHAPTER FOUR

1750

"Another tankard of ale? Or would you rather the hard cider? Harris here offers the best there is, for the location." The elderly man sitting across from the roughhewn table raised his own tankard at Tennent. Tennent shifted on the stool he straddled and replied deferentially, "If you're offering, sir. The ale please." Before Tennent shifted his wooden trencher aside, he used his mussel shell to scoop up the last pool of gravy from the venison stew, then placed the shell into the pocket of his frock coat.

Catching the attention of a young woman serving a nearby table, the man called out as his finger circled down at the table, "My dear, if you'd be so kind."

"Right away, Mr. Weiser."

Given the greetings from the crowded room, that the aforementioned Mr. Weiser received when they entered the trading post together, Tennent already figured the man was a well-respected and a familiar visitor to this establishment, accustomed to the privilege of being venerable. Their meeting had been arranged by one of the Moravian missionaries who he had been guiding through various Lenape and Shawnee encampments on the western side of the Susquehanna.

Conrad Weiser's gentle smile and bright eyes accentuated a benevolent face, softening rather than highlighting the dramatic length of his nose and his equally protruding chin. The young woman padded over to their table wearing decorative moccasins. She carried in her right hand both of the filled tankards, foam sloshing over the lips. Weiser looked at her warmly and thanked her as she bent down and placed the tankards on the table. Pipe smoke hovered toward the ceiling. She blushed at his manners, unused to being treated courteously by a gentleman of his standing, then smiled coquettishly at Tennent. Young men rarely frequented Harris' trading post.

"*Prost.*" Weiser clanked his pewter tankard against Tennent's. "Now, young man, none of this 'sir' business. I am simply a humble agent and emissary on behalf of the Provincial Government." Tennent smiled to himself at the less than subtle way Weiser reminded him of his station in life.

"Perhaps after this business in the Tuscaroras, you could accompany me to Onondaga. As Mr. Franklin of Philadelphia wrote me the other day, I have been invited to help persuade our Iroquois friends to see the . . ." Weiser paused to choose his word carefully similar to a young woman choosing the prettiest colored ribbon for her cap or the way a hunter makes sure he loads his rifle with the proper caliber bullet, ". . . the unnecessary discomfort and confusion that might arise should they accede to the . . ." again he paused to weigh his words, ". . . importunity and liberality of our generous French friends to the north. I trust we'll be successful. My friends among the Iroquois still call me by the name they gave me, *Tarachiawagon.*"

Tennent allowed himself the luxury of letting Weiser believe him impressed with Weiser's erudition, but only for a moment. "So, 'Holder of the Heavens,' once we finish with those rude Scots, you want to politely threaten the Iroquois that they had better not ally with the French."

Weiser grinned and touched the side of his pointy nose. "Precisely." He instinctively knew he had chosen the right man for the job, but he still needed to make sure. Weiser slipped briefly into his German. *Ja, wir Deutschen, mit . . .* our demeanor of obedience and compliance . . . *anders als Sie Schotte.*" We Germans prefer our world tidy, orderly, unlike you Scots. You Scot Presbyterians, well . . . you talk often enough about doing things decently and in order, but I'm surprised a brawl hasn't broken out already, given the number of your tribe here tonight."

Instead of a brawl breaking out, one of the men, who sat on a barrel at the far end of the combined trading post and tavern, started singing. Landlord Harris handed him the porchette he kept on a nearby shelf for such occasions. The man pressed it against his chest, strummed the bow against the strings, shrugged, sang a few doleful verses but quickly stopped singing. "Let's have 'Nottingham Ale' instead," he announced, "but hang the English words, boys, we'll sing it American fashion. Instead of 'Nottingham Ale,' let's call out 'John Harris' Ale' after our proud and portly proprietor! Join me, lads and lassies!"

When Venus, the goddess of beauty and love
Arose from the froth that swam on the sea
Minerva sprang out of the cranium of Jove
A coy, sullen dame as most mortals agree
But Bacchus, they tell us, that prince of good fellows
Was Jupiter's son, pray attend my tale
They who thus chatter mistake quite the matter
He sprang from a barrel of John Harris' Ale

The crowd, many with thick brogues, joined in the familiar tune, singing the chorus after each stanza.

John Harris' Ale, me boys, John Harris' Ale
No liquor on earth is like John Harris' Ale
John Harris' Ale, me boys, John Harris' Ale
No liquor on earth is like John Harris' Ale

You bishops and curates, priests, deacons and vicars
When once you have tasted, you all must agree
That John Harris' Ale is the best of all liquors
And none understands a good creature like thee.
It dispels every vapor, saves pen, ink and paper
For when you've a mind in your pulpit to rail
It'll open your throats, you may preach without notes
When inspired with a bumper of John Harris' Ale.

Ye poets who pray on the Hellican brooke
The nectar of Gods and the juice of the vine,
You say none can write well except they invoke
The friendly assistance of one of the Nine.
His liquor surpassed the streams of Parnassus
That nectar, Ambrosia, on which Gods regale
Experience will show it, naught makes a good poet
Like quantum sufficient of John Harris' Ale.

And you doctors, who more executions have done
With powder and potion and bolus and pill
Than hangman with halter, or soldier with gun
Miser with famine or lawyer with quill
To dispatch us the quicker, you forbid us malt liquor
Till our bodies consume, and our faces grow pale
Let him mind you, who pleases, what cures all diseases
A plentiful glass of good John Harris' Ale.

When he finished, a man banged his tankard and shouted at the singer, pointing toward Tennent. "How about another one for our laddie over there at the table? He's a rogue he is. Worse, he's an educated rogue. Gave up his plaid for leather-stocking. What have ye, friend, for him?"

The singer dangled his fingers across the strings pensively. The room quieted down as he played "Flowers of the Forest." Many friends long gone were remembered in the lull that followed.

After a respectful wait, a fellow dressed in hunting frock, fringed leggings, and breechclout clamored, banging his cup, "Aye, enough, enough." The woodsman reached to his neck, found and crushed an offending louse. "Ach, mate," he shouted at the musician, "a wee bit more with a giggle, will ye?"

The tune changed to a frolic. The men pounded the table in rhythm.

> Busy curious thirsty fly,
> drink with me and drink with I,
> freely welcome to my cup
> couldst thou sip and sip it up
> make the most of life you may
> life is short and wears away
> life is short and wears away
> life is short and wears away

As the singing continued and turned increasingly ribald, Conrad Weiser rocked on his stool and soaked in the refreshing fellowship of these leather-stocking, rustic frontiersmen. "Nothing like it," he said. He reached over and tapped the back of Tennent's hand. "If you're done, let's go outside to the mulberry tree for a talk." Weiser collected his tricorn and placed coins in the young woman's hand, who curtsied in thanks, then navigated his way through the crowd toward the low door. Tennent gathered up his kit and rifle, tugged his floppy hat onto his head, and followed Weiser outside.

They stood beneath the mulberry tree. Weiser patted it. "Harris," he said, "loves to tell the story of when some renegades tied his father to this tree and prepared to commit all sorts of indignities upon him before they burnt him alive. Have you heard this story before?"

Weiser didn't wait for Tennent to answer. "Not sure which tribe. They demanded rum. Probably Shawnees. The Shawnees have a taste for it, and it causes plenty of problems, thanks to some of our less scrupulous traders. Well, Harris, being one of the good ones, refused them the rum. Lucky for him, his slave Hercules rowed across the Susquehanna to recruit the help of some friendlier Indians and effected a rescue. A grateful Harris freed Hercules then and there. So Harris Junior tells it."

Continued Weiser, pointing out the tombstone under the tree with the name burnt into it. "This is Harris' grave. The father died two years ago. Insisted on being buried under this tree, beside his homestead that he and his wife built here out of nothing." He looked at Tennent in the light of the almost full moon. The river sparkled where the current splashed. Weiser's tone turned quieter, deeper, authoritative. "Where, Tennent, do you expect to be buried? Will your body go back to your family in Philadelphia, to the famous Tennents? Yes, I know most of your story, you and your erstwhile academic career. But what I need to know is whether you are a boy whose readings filled him with romantic fantasies, who now seeks an adventure so you can go home the hero and brag about it to your friends or to a special lady? Or are you a dilettante, playing at common woodsman to impress yourself? Or are you some self-flagellating hermit seeking escape and atonement because of a bitterness or disappointment, or because some weight of guilt has driven you away from the company of mankind?"

Tennent laughed, which was not the reaction Weiser anticipated. "I thought I gave up sitting for examinations when I left College two years ago." Tennant chuckled freely. "You say you know my story. Fine, there's little to tell. I love academics, I loved the learning, I loved how books— all kinds of books—fed my intellect and grew my mind. You say you know my story. Then you tell me. Tell me how I simply left College and headed west." He remembered how he had thought his father would be angry with him, especially since his father was proud of being one of the founders of the College. Yes, Father had been disappointed. He hadn't been angry though, nor especially surprised.

There was only one thing for which Tennent had asked his father's permission, provided his father's new wife, Cornelia, wouldn't mind. He had asked for a keepsake of his late mother. Cornelia had agreed. She had been kind enough to let him take his mother's embroidery scissors from her sewing basket. Then, Father, after making some suggestions about colleagues serving in parishes along the Octorara and in Lancaster, had offered a prayer in parting.

Tennent looked back at Weiser and met his eyes. "The mind isn't the only part of us humans that needs to be fed. Nor is the belly the only part that needs to be fed. The heart too, between mind and belly, must be fed."

Weiser stepped back a pace, feeling vulnerable before this young man. He suddenly wondered if his life had been spent conforming to the expectations of others, especially of those important and influential. "Come, Weiser, negotiate this treaty. Come to this council and translate. Come, persuade the Delawares to accept our purchase of their land. Come to Onondaga and convince the Iroquois to stop the raids south. Come, and with your skills, convince the ten tribes to relinquish their rights to the Ohio Valley while we start building forts." His had been a life of important duty. So why was he feeling envious of this young man's ardor?

"You want me to tell you where I want to be buried? Really?" asked Tennent, suppressing a desire to scoff. "Sir, you make a common mistake about us Presbyterians and our view of predestination. The wrong view is that we believe in fate. That God had somehow decreed that John Harris, Senior, would be buried beneath a mulberry tree. That God has decreed that I, Alexander Tennent, will fall to a tomahawk or will fall asleep in a goose down bed and cross over. That sounds more like Zeus than God." Tennant laughed again. "Stuff and nonsense. What we believe is to trust God. Trust that our God is our protector, the defender of mankind, and that, whatever comes our way when we continue in the way, all will be well. All will be well, regardless. 'Regardless' is the faith part in all this."

"Theologian too, now," joked Weiser weakly.

Tennent leaned on his rifle. "So, Mr. Weiser, humble agent and emissary of the Provincial Government, did I pass the examination? Not that I particularly care whether I did or not. That was one of the problems between me and the Reverend Burr at the College of New Jersey. I wanted to learn, not be required to echo what the examiners wanted to hear. Save that for the catechism."

Weiser wasn't sure how to respond. It sounded like defiance. It also sounded like honest confidence. Again, Weiser felt vulnerable. He preferred being in charge.

"Not particularly deferential, are you?"

"That's what Burr said."

"Are you sure you're a preacher's son?"

"Raised to be respectful. Deference, however, wears like a tight pair of boots."

Weiser pursed his lips.

After a long and apprehensive silence beneath the mulberry tree, Tennent decided to offer, symbolically, the first puff of the peace-pipe and ratification of a treaty. He reached out his hand to Weiser. "If you still want me to go, I will go. Whither thou goest. I still think you are hanging your hat on an elk's tail. I think it a fool's errand, but if you don't mind another fool, I'll go."

Weiser looked at Tennent's outstretched hand before deciding to shake it. "You may be young, but it's obvious you are no tyro, no novice. One thing I ask you, scout, is don't let them—whether Oneida or Delaware or Shawnee or Cayuga—know that you know their tongue. It helps in case you overhear things they don't want us to hear. You don't speak German, do you? No? If we want to confuse them, we can speak a little Latin. This applies especially for the Shikellamies who'll be joining us in a few days along the Juniata. I've been told you are familiar with the Juniata, yes?"

"Yes," Tennent replied.

Weiser continued, "These Shikellamies have been deputized by the new leader, the newest appointed sachem of Shamokin Village, Shikellamy's own son—God rest my old friend's soul—on behalf of the Iroquois. You should know that they don't trust us to carry out our task."

"Would you?" asked Tennent with a wry smile.

Weiser screwed up his face, clucked his tongue, and rubbed his chin. "When it comes to us dealing with those infernal Scotch-Irish squatters, I trust you can help interpret their unfathomable brand of English. Remind them how we are trying to avoid a war. We are trying to save their lives."

Tennent replied in Gaelic. "*Bhiodh e na urram dhomh.*"

"Translation please," sighed Weiser.

"It would be my honor."

CHAPTER FIVE

1750

The other members of the delegation, George Crogham, Justice of the Peace, and Richard Peters, secretary of the Provincial Council, arrived on horseback two days later. Neither man, nor their aides, were strangers to the frontier. All, except Weiser, carried arms: pistols, Lancaster rifles like Tennent's, and several muskets. Tennent was puzzled why Barabbas Cromwell, the stout Under-Sherriff, carried a blunderbuss. Cromwell later explained, "You hunters want accuracy. Me? I deal with mobs at close hand. I want to scare Beelzebub himself out of them." He patted the short barrel. "This'll do it."

Do what exactly, thought a brooding Tennent. *This man has the stink of gallows about him.*

The path of their expedition was simple, as they traced it on the map rolled out onto a table in the trading post. "We'll take Harris' Ferry to the western bank of the Susquehanna, hike up to the mouth of the Juniata, track the path of the river inland. When the river veers northwest, we head due south through the Tuscarora valley. Our scout here knows the trails."

Said Tennent, "If we stayed traveling upstream, we'd come to the Onayutta, the source for the name for this river."

"Our destination is a hamlet called Sidneysville," continued Weiser pointing toward a spot at the bottom of the map. He looked up at Peters. "Sidneysville, correct?" Peters nodded. "After we are done there, we wind through the gap, find the Frankstown Path and head back to Harris' Ferry for some warm hospitality. We complete the circuit."

One of the aides pulled on his beard and asked, "The Onayutta? What is that?"

"Tell them, Tennent," instructed Weiser, "what the Onayutta is. You're the one familiar with the country."

Tennent complied. "It means Standing Stone in Oneida, located about ten miles from that bend." He tapped the spot on the map. "It's over twice the size of a tall man. The Oneida, you might have heard, are the people of the standing stone. Stone pillars, they say, fell from the sky to mark that this is where they belong, their sacred land. Of course, the Lenape, the Tuscarora, the Shawnee all claim rights to the land. As I said, we call the river the Juniata, our anglicized version of Onayutta." Tennent sucked his teeth, glancing over at Weiser. "Like the Germans, we write Js where they don't belong. Unlike the Germans, we like the sound of the J."

"Ja. Continue please, school master."

"It's worth the visit. The stone probably goes back to the original natives, given the stories carved into it. I stayed among the people there a while. I was privileged to make friends with a few Susquehannocks, who also were permitted to stay there a while."

"Which is one reason why I've asked Tennent to join us," said Weiser.

"There's similar carvings south of here, on some rocks in the Susquehanna that you can see when the river is low," Tennent added invitingly. "We leave our marks to tell our stories. Thunderbird spirit. Manitou spirit. Transformed human figure. Walking bird. Serpent shape. Tracks of bear, elk, deer, bird."

Peters interrupted. "Lenape, Tuscarora, Shawnee. And now the bloody Scots leaving their mark and staking claim on where they don't belong." Peters rapped the map with his knuckles. "May I remind you gentlemen why we are here, on behalf of the Deputy Governor of the Province. Hamilton didn't commission us to ramble on about admiring pagan artifacts."

Tennent, chastened and silenced, drifted away from the table.

* * *

It rained the morning of their departure. Tennent, hoisting his haversack over one shoulder, his gourd of water bumping against his back, took his turn boarding the raft for the expedition's first trip across the Susquehanna. The watery stretch between Harris' Ferry and the opposite shore was a mile, the Susquehanna being deepest and widest at this point.

From his travels south, Tennent found it curious how the Susquehanna funneled down just before its mouth at the Chesapeake. He double-checked the leather wrappings covering his rifle's lock. The river, muddy and turbid as usual, had increased its current due to the rainfall. Tennent figured they'd have to add another mile to their fifteen-mile hike to the mouth of the Juniata.

The raftsmen poled alternatively to fight against the push of the current and avoid losing forward momentum. Finally reaching the western shore, they disembarked a mile below the sloping landing. Two hours later, the full party assembled and walked sulkily upriver toward the landing, where they turned into the woods to find the trail. Tennent periodically removed his floppy hat and shook it. Those wearing Tricorns simply leaned forward and let the water drain out. Single file, like the Lenape, they headed north along the narrow trail toward the mouth of the Juniata, where, due to the rain and delay at the ferry, they made first camp, disturbing a heron which launched itself elegantly away from them.

Awakened by the gentle call of a mourning dove—coo-ah, coo, coo, coo—Tennent stirred before the others and performed his morning routine: Shake off the Pennsylvania dew and chill, unwrap the leather straps around his rifle's lock, check flint, open frizzen, thumb out the damp powder, clean out the touch hole, prime the pan with fresh powder, close frizzen. With his weapon ready, he paced about the camp's perimeter.

Coo-ah, coo, coo, coo, repeated the mourning dove. Two rabbits started, scampering off to safety. Gray squirrels pranced and scampered. Finding all as quiet as the dawn allows, except for the sounds of men at restless sleep, he reached for a branch of a maple tree, bent it, tugged off a twig. With his knife, he honed it of leaves, sliced a series of slits in the end, flattened it with his knife against a stone, and began scrubbing his teeth with this chewstick. He looked around for some sage or mint. Imitating the Delaware rather than most of the woodsmen he'd met, he wanted to keep his teeth.

With no success finding dry wood, breakfast consisted of dried beef and Harris' pickled eggs. No griddled scrapple this day. Expecting to forage, hunt, and fish—part of Tennent's duties as scout—there had been no need to pack and carry sufficient viands for the entire journey. Gnats swarmed over the water, hinting at good fishing. An egret strolled along the river's edge. Tennent admired this lazy, slumbering Juniata, deeper and wider than all the tributaries of the Susquehanna he'd seen, much of its length shaded by thick foliage. *It's the tributaries that form the river.* Tennent never could decide if the West Branch farther north could be rightfully considered a tributary. Tennent knew that farther upstream by leagues, Juniata's rifts and rocks, the shallow water, would appear. It would be easier there to harvest eels for their meal, catching them and rolling down their skin the way a Philadelphia gentleman removed his stockings. There would be weirs where the smaller creeks flowed into the Juniata.

* * *

The expedition sighted the first cluster of settlers early the third day. They heard the commotion coming from that direction before they came upon the shacks. Three white men were arguing with three Indians, whose paint indicated that they were Iroquois. A fourth Iroquois, peculiarly wearing a hunting shirt, leaned against an oak tree.

"Ah," exclaimed Weiser, putting his hand on Tennent's shoulder, "I see our Shikellamies have preceded us and begun negotiations." He turned toward Clapham and Peters. "These are the representatives from Shamokin Village we were supposed to rendezvous with yesterday."

The shouting from both sides intensified. Gestures were offered, but each side kept their distance and avoided touching the other. The Iroquois brave standing off to the side watched in silence. Looking over his shoulder, Tennent saw Sherriff Cromwell raise his blunderbuss across his chest.

"We had better intervene," suggested Weiser. He signaled for Tennent. "Come with me. And remember, just listen."

Two women stood in front of a ripped blanket that served as a door for one of the shacks. Their drab wraparound skirts were tattered and torn at the bottom. Neither woman wore a cap. Two children wearing sackcloth stood still and watched the confrontation. When the women saw Weiser's party approach, they grabbed the children and ducked behind the blanket.

Addressing them first in Oneida, then in English, Weiser tried to calm them down. Recognizing Weiser, the Shikellamies backed up. Weiser introduced himself to the settlers and announced that he was a representative of the Provincial Government; and had orders to evict all settlers in violation of the treaty signed with the Iroquois Confederacy.

"This is their hunting grounds," explained Weiser to them. "They have full rights to it." Tennent retreated a few paces and listened as the three Iroquois confided to each other how pleased they were that the white man's government had paid attention to their complaints. One of the three shook his head, saying he regretted that Weiser had arrived when he did. "We could have handled these men. We could have handled this problem without so much talk." Tennent turned his head toward them. The other two nodded and touched their tomahawks. Tennent, hoping he hadn't betrayed himself, pretended to look past them.

"You're defending these damned Indians," yelled one of the squatters. "No one's going to force me off my land." At a beckoning gesture from Secretary Peters, Cromwell pressed his hand on Tennent's shoulder, shoved himself in front of him, and stepped toward the angry man. Cromwell thumbed the flint to make sure it was tight and lowered the blunderbuss at the man, who sneered at the Under-Sherriff. Peters pulled several papers from a pouch and waved them.

"I have the authority and the responsibility. I am the government agent. You are squatters. We will evict you by whatever force is necessary. We'll truss you up and cart you off to the gaol in Lancaster if necessary. We will stay here for the night and see you off in the morning."

One of the angry squatter's friends pulled him by the arm, while another jumped in front of him and faced him, encouraging him to back away. "Ye canna win. Robbie, ye canna win," this man repeated. The three Iroquois, familiar enough with English, looked smug and satisfied. The fourth displayed no emotion; but watched Tennent from the corner of his eye.

Over the next days, as they traveled down the valley accompanied by the four Shikellamies, more evictions were ordered. Weiser was getting increasingly nettled by their complaints. To him, these ignorant borderers were in the wrong. They were annoying, endangering themselves, inflaming the entire frontier. Weiser was offended when one settler accused them of being Philadelphia aristocrats, arguing that they were going to cheat the Indians anyway and sell the land for themselves. "We came from nothing, now you're making sure we get less than nothing," blamed a frustrated settler.

As the resistance increased, so increased the governmental browbeating, as Peters resented the settler's rebellious refusal to respect his position and his person.

A wife, clutching her infant, screamed and spat at them, "Where are we supposed to go? My babies need a home. Where next? You already told us we had to move out of the Octorara region." Her infant started crying, and two toddlers held onto her skirt.

Her friend shouted shrilly, "Your Deputy Governor told us he wanted us to build up this area."

Her husband joined in. "I have proof. I purchased this land from a land agent!" He raced inside his cabin and returned, showing Weiser the signed receipt. Tennent leaned in and tried to read the paper. Weiser turned to Clapham. "*Gott helfe uns*," he sighed. "The man can't read; it's a bill of sale from last year for a bullock."

Tennent withdrew. At each of the confrontations with the settlers, he tried to linger near the Shikellamies, partly because with each eviction he wanted less and less to be complicit, partly because he had his own suspicions. He realized that the Shikellamies were playing the same game he was. For two of them, their English was better than they let on. Most of what they said to each other was sparse, typical of their culture's stoicism. Sometimes they would question one another whether or not some of the settler's stories rang true, or if the Provincial Government had plans other than those agreed to with the Iroquois. Tennent suspected seeds of dangerous doubt were being planted. He sensed that when they reached Sidneysville, purported to be center of the squatters, they would want proof of Weiser's commitment to the Iroquois' rights to their land. The fourth Shikellamie, Tennent noticed, never spoke.

* * *

They found Sidneysville to be a colony of eleven squatters. Once they got them removed, their expedition could boast the evictions of over sixty squatters since heading south from the Juniata. Weiser, Peters, and Clapham felt justified and convinced that theirs was an important work. Treaties were being enforced. Settlers who might otherwise be attacked by war parties were being shepherded back east toward safety. They congratulated each other.

The Sidneysville settlers didn't agree. The bad news had already reached them. They were ready and waiting. They rejected the term squatter. All they wanted was opportunity. All they wanted was a chance for a farm and a life and a taste of prosperity, which they weren't able to receive in the communities east of the Susquehanna. They weren't asking for much. As they figured it, since they never saw an Indian settle in the Tuscarora Valley, the Indians didn't own it either. Despite Weiser trying to lecture them, it never occurred to these squatters that the Iroquois concept of ownership and that of the Shawnee, Leni Lenape, and Oneida, might differ from theirs. The way Tennent figured it, it could have been worked out. *It's the authorities who are getting in the way*, he believed. He began to suspect there were other invisible hands at play here that neither Weiser nor the Shikellamies could see; although the suspicions of the Shikellamies might have more merit, given experience.

"How do you hold back the tide?" Tennent had asked of Weiser the night before they arrived at Sidneysville. "How do you hold back imagination and ambition? These people are hungry. I know where they came from, from huts in the Scottish highlands, stone and sod. None it is fair. What happens when you try to block a trail of ants in the forest? They find another way to go around, don't they?"

Peters confronted the colony, thrusting his warrant at them. "Pack up now," he demanded.

They refused. One man aimed his rifle at Weiser and ordered him to turn tail and leave. Sherriff Cromwell grunted and pointed his blunderbuss at the crowd of men, women, and children. "Surrender your weapon or I unload," he threatened. It sounded to Tennent as if Cromwell was enjoying this. The man looked around at the women and children. He glared back at the blunderbuss, finally lowering the rifle barrel as Peters' aides rushed to restrain him.

The Shikellamies said something to Weiser that made Tennent wince in pain. He glared at Weiser. "I didn't come here to burn up what little these desperate people have. It's not them who need to be restrained. I didn't sign up for this. This isn't justice. This is far from righteous."

Weiser tried to explain. "It's for the best, best for them. Peace requires sacrifices. Sherriff," Weiser ordered, "Get a torch."

Sherriff Cromwell rushed inside one of the cabins, picked up a broom, wrapped it in a shawl that he found folded on top of a bench, and shoved it into the fireplace. He emerged with it upraised and burning. Peters ordered, "You have ten minutes to remove your belongings."

Tennent rushed to wrest the torch from the Sherriff's hand. "You can't," he protested. Cromwell twisted away, grazing Tennant's arm with the flames. Two of the aides shoved Tennent to the ground. Tennent, clutching his rifle in his right hand, rolled into a kneeling position, prepared swing his rifle butt against his shoulder.

"You point that at me," threatened Cromwell, "and you are dead." Tennent looked around. Pistols were aimed at him.

"I'm done. I'm ashamed. I'm done with you all," he seethed, as he turned his back on them, grabbed his kit, and headed toward the woods.

The Shikellamie who hadn't spoken a word the entire time followed him into the woods. "Righteous One," he called out to Tennent in Oneida.

"What do you want?" he replied angrily in the same language, pivoting to confront the man.

"I knew you could speak Oneida," he said softly. "Please, I am your friend. Let there be no cloud between us." Tennent breathed heavily; then relaxed, eased, and relented.

The brave continued. "You haven't heard me speak, because I too am ashamed. I am the youngest son of the great Shikellamy. I am called Sogogeghyata. My name is Cayuga because my mother was Cayuga. My brother Sayughtowa is full of vengeance and fire. You heard him demanding that we burn those people out." Sogogeghyata spat. "In English, he is called Beetling Brow, because he always sees others as potential enemies. He treats white men as the white man treats us. But he sees only the ones filled with hate. He hasn't looked for men like you. He says he learned this hate by watching how your people treat your own kind."

Tennent reached out and placed his hand on Sogogeghyata's shoulder.

Sogogeghyata placed his right hand on Tennent's shoulder. "Who is just these days? Yet do not these days need men who are just?"

Tennent studied Sogogeghyata's eyes before answering. "I once heard one of your people sing a song of your father, how he was a well-spoken man, a man of peace, a man who held off the bloodshed. Yes, I believe you are just."

"My brothers are not, which is why I had to come and see."

"My brothers also are not, though they believe they are."

"We are the same then. We speak of righteousness, a word my father learned when he became a Christian, shortly before he died of the fever. It was a new word for us, but a meaning important to us as well."

"I, too, am Christian." Tennent said intimately. "Many of us speak the word you speak, yet too few know the power of the word."

"Take this, as a gift and as a sign of hope for our people." Sogogeghyata pulled a tomahawk from his belt and handed it to Tennent. The blade was iron, the handle ash, unadorned except for three metal inlays. "Should you visit my father's village, show it to my eldest brother Tachnech-toris," he said. "He is now leader in the Long House, and you will be welcomed," he added, before returning to the cabins.

Hitching his haversack over his shoulder, Tennent walked north, carrying all he owned as the flames crackled.

CHAPTER SIX

1750

It took Tennent months of trudging through the wilderness until he felt clean again. He wanted to stay away from humans, regardless the skin of their tribe. Leaving Weiser's party to themselves, he backtracked the Tuscarora path, pausing to note the abandoned shacks. With his gear stored on a makeshift raft, he swam across the Onayutta, then, coming to the next big tributary north, he waded through the Kaarondinhah, rifle and powder held high. Keeping on the west bank of the river, he came to where the two branches of the Susquehanna merged, where he located the trace that eventually would eventually veer away from the west branch of the Susquehanna toward that great upstream island named Mechek-menatey and head into the western hills. Instead, several miles north of the confluence, he noticed where two islands afforded an easy crossing over to the east bank. The scout paused, smiled, and shrugged. He set up camp and prepared to cross over in the morning. He remembered a rumor he had once heard, and a story her had heard from an old trapper. He also never had traveled that east side before.

When he first started out to learn the frontier a trapper, his face leathery, his arms scarred, permitted him to share his campfire one night where the Octorara entered into the Susquehanna. Feeding twigs into the fire, the trapper spoke in reverent tones about an important village called Otston-wakin, located at the mouth of the Lawi-saquick where the West Branch elbowed abruptly westward. "Otstonwakin," the man repeated, "a trading center, home for hundreds."

The trapper continued, "Oddly enough, a woman had been their chief. She of mixed blood. A strange story, eh? What was her name? Yes, they called her Madam Montour, she believed to be of French and Algonquin mix, or possibly a French captive daughter raised Algonquin." He sipped water from his gourd. "Always wanted to visit there." He paused, surprised at having spoken so many words. "Stories along the river, young fellow, say that one day the place just vanished." The trapper concluded, "She was considered a great chief."

That night, rolling himself up in his bedroll, an intrigued Tennent entertained himself with the name the trapper mentioned. Montoir in French. To mount. A mountain. A horse is a mount. To mount a horse, you step on a horseblock, a little mountain. Well, what did it matter? Like his own name, perhaps, Montour was given by circumstance more than by lineage. My name? Tennent. Probably my people were tenant farmers scraping and bowing and starving before some lord of the manor. Strange, how we end up with our names. Before drifting to sleep, he wondered what became of her.

The two islands made his crossing easy. Following the bank of the eastern shore on the parallel trail, he headed toward this Lawi-saquick. After two days, he arrived at the Lawi-saquick. Wading over at a ford above the mouth, he entered a space obviously cleared by man. It was cluttered with abandoned wigwams, collapsed drying racks, unused campfires, fields of squash, corn, beans grown wild, and a small trash heap of mussel shells and fragments of pottery. "Could this be Otstonwakin?" Tennant asked aloud, as if to receive an answer. "What ghosts and legends here?" Only the wind and riffling water answered. The place was indeed deserted. No sign of corpses. What happened here, he wondered. Was it war? Was it disease, as in too many other villages? Where did the people go? Those who had the luck to survive? Those who could adapt? Those fittest for some reason?Maybe they fled west, away from a contagion from which they had no defense.

These questions were beyond him. Tennent pulled on his moustache. He laughed to himself about his own easy melancholy. "Grasping ghosts again," he muttered, as he picked up a charred, broken tree limb covered in splotches of chalky white growth and flung it aside. Earth to earth, ashes to ashes, dust to dust. Did anyone deliver a eulogy, or at least offer a committal, for Otstonwakin?

* * *

Rumors of this strange man wandering alone through the woods were spread by the braves whispering to each other along the trails, and back around the campfire. They talked of the man with two tomahawks.

One Lenape brave reported seeing him take position behind a tree and aim at an elk, its velvet antlers sprouting into points already. The thirsty bull had drifted from the herd near the arched shape tree, a familiar trail marker tree, to step into the cool waters to lap from the Sinnemahoning, the Rocky Lick. The brave told how he watched the man with two tomahawks three times raise his rifle and prepare to kill the elk. Three times the woodsman lowered his rifle and shook his head. From his hiding place in the thicket, the Lenape brave saw the woodsman quietly retreat and leave the great elk in peace. He couldn't understand him refusing to shoot. Such a kill would bring honor to him for feeding his people. "Perhaps," said an elder that night to the Lenape brave, "he will not kill when there is no reason. Perhaps he has no people to feed, only himself."

Another man, a brave of the Cayugas, spread the story of how he saw this man with two tomahawks standing alone on the shore, where the Erie-lhonan people once fished this vast fresh water sea before they too disappeared. As the tribe of the Erie-lhonan ebbed, other tribes swelled and filled their place along the shores of the great lake that all newcomers still called by their name: Erie-lhonan. The Cayuga brave watched as the strange woodsman quietly leaned on his rifle and watched men from the nearby village out in their canoes, tossing out their nets weighted with stones, dragging them, then hauling them up between the canoes. The man with two tomahawks simply watched, as walleye and bluegill tumbled into one of the dugouts. At one point, he seemed to wipe his eyes.

A Seneca boy went out to prove himself a warrior by showing he did not fear the stories said of this wandering white man. The boy described how one evening he silently walked into the man's camp. On a spit over his fire, two pheasants roasted. The Seneca boy squatted near the fire. No words were exchanged. When the pheasants were done and cooled, the white man gestured to the boy that he should eat. Together they dined in silence. They shared a cup of berries. As the fire flickered, two hazel-colored eyes glowed from the darkness beyond the light of the fire. The boy knew they were the eyes of a lynx. He watched as the man stared back at the eyes, then pulled out, from his haversack, his housewife and quietly repaired his moccasins. The next day the white man rose, readied his rifle, gathered his kit, and walked south into the gap of the mountain range ten miles from the headwaters of the Alleghene, due south from where the Ischue, a large creek, entered the Alleghene. The boy followed silently.

After a winding, steep, five-mile ascent toward the summit, mist hovering in various valleys below them, the white man stopped, removed his hat, and ran his fingers through his hair. In front of him appeared a city of boulders in various shapes, sizes, and positions. Tree and shrubs grew where they could. Moss covered portions of the rock face. The man whistled in admiration of the terrain, surprising the boy, though the boy didn't admit that part in the telling of the tale. Nor did he mention his fear when coming upon this mysterious place. But the white man began exploring, walking through the cramped passages. The white man simply grinned wide and stretched out both arms as he rested his rifle against a boulder and pressed the palms of his hands against the sides of one passageway. The man continued on, admiring the stone arches, climbing toward boulders which appeared to teeter, and ready to tumble were they touched, and mounting rock outcroppings that were easily the height of two oak trees, to survey the mountain range surrounding them. By that time the mists had cleared. The boy had heard his elders tell of legends of giants tossing rocks at each other, more in play than anger. This must be such a place. The boy was nervous and apprehensive, but he dared not show how he felt. He was a Seneca brave and would act like a Seneca brave.

The man made camp there that night and again the boy joined him. They shared a tea of mint leaves boiled in his cup. Come next morning, the boy awakened to discover he was alone.

CHAPTER SEVEN

1750–1751

Tennent sniffed the wind. The omens were all around, starting with honking geese. Buck rubs had been obvious for weeks now, the tree bark peeled and ripped, the bucks rubbing off the velvet to toughen up their antlers for the competition to follow. The apple skins were tougher, the cornhusks drier. The berries were still plentiful. Tennent reached down and picked up a wooly bear caterpillar, then gently placed it back on the fallen leaves. The omens predicting a cold winter were strong. The caterpillar's band was small in comparison to its black front and back—depending, Tennent smiled, on which part exactly is the back and which is the front. The trees had begun to paint themselves from autumn's palette, soon a riot of color, then the dormancy, the months of rest approaching. Daylight was shortening, darkness lengthening. The glistening morning dew turned frosty, the decoration of morning hoarfrost. The squirrels were scrambling and chirping faster and louder, excited by this year's acorn mast, signaling the oak tree's yearning to propagate, to outpace predation, the chilling gusts shaking the bounty loose. The bachelor groups of the young bucks were breaking apart, their antlers thickening and hardening, the bucks going their separate ways. Their youthful sparring was turning into the rougher competition for the does, which hadn't yet begun bleating. Soon the bucks would turn reckless, randy with the rutting rage—eyes rolled back, nostrils flaring, smelling, catching scent, scraping, urinating, marking. Grunt, grunt. Tap, tap, tap, uh, uh, uh.

Friend bear finds shelter. So must I. He touched the handle of one of his tomahawks and started walking south toward Susquehanna's West Branch to pick up the path that would lead him to Shamokin Village.

* * *

Imagination can be cruel. Imagined expectations can be crueler. Arriving at Shamokin Village reminded him of when he had arrived at the Reverend Burr's Newark manse in 1747 to join the handful of students attending the College of New Jersey. Encouraged by his father's respect for Burr, Tennent had looked forward to the sophisticated level of conversation, the serious debate over critical subjects in Natural Philosophy. Should we regard the Westminster Standards as a guide, or must those ordained adopt it entirely? What are the indispensable marks of a Christian? What are the dangers, as father preached, about unconverted clergy? Alexander had known he carried into college his father's reputation. He had studied intensively his classics, keen on memorizing witty quotations in Latin and Greek to impress his fellow students with his wit and banter.

College. The name said it all: 'collegium,' a society of learned colleagues intent on academic excellence and intellectual rigor. His young enthusiasm imagined how Newark could rival the Athenian Academy, waistcoats and buttoned breeches instead of togas, tricorns instead of laurel wreaths. There were Harvard and Yale for the New Englanders, William and Mary for the Virginians. Now, courtesy of his grandfather, father, uncles, and their friends, they could boast of the College of New Jersey as a site for classical education for the yearning, common sense middle.

That was the expectation, the dream.

The reality was instead dingy rooms, tedious lectures, moralistic admonitions, strict regulations, painfully long prayers, longer sermons, and a beggar's library.

Imagination can be cruel. Imagined expectations can be crueler.

* * *

Shamokin Village was reputed to house over three hundred families, safe in their wigwams, gathered inside a stockade. Oneida, Delaware, Shawnee, even a few remaining Susquehannocks lived together there in peace. Shamokin Village grew to be a flourishing trading village, fed by trail and river, which the Iroquois governed. The Iroquois chiefs appointed those sachems who acted on their behalf, such as Shikellamy, and now his son, who went by different names depending on which of his aims the name best served: John Shikellamy, or John Logan or, in Oneida, Tachnechtoris, meaning, The Spreading Oak.

Tennent arrived hoping to reconnect with Shikellamy's youngest son, Sogogeghyata, once he got permission to enter the Long House and introduce himself. Weiser, he later was told, had built this Long House as a gift for Shikellamy, complete with shingled roof. It had the effect Weiser intended, an endorsement to the villagers that Shikellamy was the appointed chief. Now it was Tachnechtoris.

"Do you wish to speak in English or Oneida," asked Tachnechtoris.

"This is your home, and I am the visitor," replied Tennant, speaking in Oneida.

"What is it that you wish from us?"

"Before I answer, let me tell you that your brother, Sogogeghyata, and I became friends months ago." Tennent removed from his belt the tomahawk with the ash handle and three metal inlays. "He gave me this tomahawk as a gift of our friendship."

"Yes, it was my father's gift to my brother." Tennant noticed that Tachnechtoris began to move his upturned hand out toward Tennant, then steadied it. "A gift from my brother is my gift to you. What now do you bring to us?"

"Only my need for safety and warmth through the winter." Tennent relaxed and rested his rifle's butt on the ground between his feet. "Along with my skill to hunt with your hunting parties and bring in meat for those who are hungry. I had long looked forward to hunting with your brother."

Tachnectoris nodded, saying, "We will take of our own people, my brother's friend." He paused. "But you will not find my brother here. He has traveled beyond the Ohi-yo after the second full moon of the summer, and we do not know when he may return."

"I am saddened that I have missed him."

"For my brother's sake, you are welcome, although some of my braves are weary of you English traveling amongst us. It would be best if you would seek to introduce yourself to my father's Moravians. You will find them at the mission church my father gave them permission to build." With that, Tennant was dismissed.

The Moravians confirmed to him, that, yes, there was flourishing trade at Shamokin Village; sadly, mostly trade in refugee Indians and rum. The Moravians treated Tennent cautiously at first. They became more cordial when Tennent mentioned the names of a few of the Moravian missionaries he had assisted during his first days along the frontier. They invited him to sit and take a cup of cider.

Their leader, John Martin Mack, apologized. "Forgive us, neighbor, for our own growing worries make us apprehensive of all visitors. Too many frontiersmen have come into the village, and make big promises, trading pelts for rum. This shouldn't surprise you, but trouble comes when these trappers come."

Mack's wife, Jeannette, added, "Fortunately, these men, hungry for worldly food, rarely visit long, and none stay."

"True,' Mack continued. "Most settlers prefer to press west into the Tuscarora Mountains and farther beyond, or they wish to migrate upstream on either branch of the Susquehanna." Tennent pursed his lips and nodded. He remembered warning Weiser about trying to stop ants.

The missionaries showed him around Shamokin Village. "See there," Mack pointed, "there's the other Long House, that's where Chief Allumapees lived. His Long House once was a fine home. But now, similar to the village itself, it is deteriorating. Allumapees was a decent sachem until he took to drink. It's a scourge. Isn't this why our Lord sent us here?" he asked. Tennent sensed that they said this because they needed to remind themselves of their reason for remaining. He admired them. Instantly he remembered his mother's favorite Psalm, the Psalm he quoted often enough during his travels:

> I will lift up mine eyes unto the hills
> from whence cometh my help.
> My help cometh even from the Lord
> who hath made heaven and earth.

He will not suffer thy foot to be moved
and he that keepeth thee will not sleep.
Behold, he that keepeth Israel
shall neither slumber nor sleep.

The Lord himself is thy keeper
the Lord is thy defence upon thy right hand;
So that the sun shall not burn thee by day
neither the moon by night.

The Lord shall preserve thee from all evil
yea, it is even he that shall keep thy soul.
The Lord shall preserve thy going out, and thy
    coming in
from this time forth for evermore.

"My wife and I plan to leave soon, but others will be here, others will arrive," promised Mack. "Yet, other missionaries come through here who, I grieve, lack the gift and spirit. They see these people under this curse, and they judge them as wicked and dissolute heathens, then they shake the dust from their feet and peddle on to preach among the settlements."

Tennent grimaced, guessing the names of some of these missionaries. His father once read to him a portion of a letter David Brainerd wrote about his missionary work out in this "hideous and howling wilderness." Brainerd had been influenced by his father's preaching. For Tennent, this vivid description whetted his appetite to venture out to discover this hideous and howling wilderness. So, too, another line in the letter; how when Brainerd wrote how he met Shikellamy and sought to evangelize Shamokin Village, Brainerd described he had "little satisfaction by reason of the heathenish dance and revelry they held within the house where I was obliged to lodge." Perhaps in an odd way, Tennent weighed in his mind, Brainerd's words planted the seed that brought him here. He remembered how his father carefully folded up the letter and remarked, "The Lord made divine use of David's short and troubled life."

"These poor people, so ill used, find it useful to blame us. Some threaten us, despite them wanting our traders to bring them what's ruining them." Mack paused before enfolding his palms around Tennent's right hand. "Stay the winter if you wish; but understand there is a growing climate of hostility and resentment here. They won't even let us keep our own livestock."

Tennent recalled when an old woodsman, over several tankards at Harris' Ferry after a month of trapping together, had warned him: "When a people are abused, they act like an abused people." The old woodsman cocked his eye at Tennent, then looked down at his own feet and pointed to the water spaniel curled at his moccasins. "You've seen on the trail, Tennent, how my dog loves me. Why? Because I love him. I've known men to beat their dogs to make them obey. Damn be it all, life is too short and wears too thin too fast. Mistreating a dog only makes a good hound snarl or growl so much they beat the dog out of him. Same with my two boys when they were young, God rest their souls. Beating a boy only makes him mean or submissive. Either way, you end up beating what's good out of him. Ain't no good, ain't no good."

* * *

Tennent discovered more about Shamokin Village soon enough. The wooly bears had predicted a harsh winter. Their prognostication proved correct. Along with the cold winter came food shortages, snowfalls and persistent frosts, and high winds. Were it not for Anton the blacksmith, and his wife Catharina, winter would have been colder and crueler for Tennent. He, courtesy of the Moravians who brokered an arrangement with Anton, likely enjoyed the warmest berth in Shamokin, next to the forge, board earned for work. Tennent became a contented indentured servant, pumping the bellows as needed. Often, he earned his keep handing tools to Anton—hammer, tongs—when there were fry pans, axes, horseshoes, and hoes for Anton to repair. No charge for the Lenape. That was the agreement with the chief. The Moravians could work a blacksmith shop and spread the gospel. The price? No charge to the Lenape for what came from anvil and forge. Ordinarily, the forge was fed by charcoal, but timber was becoming scarce. The earth can offer up only so many mature trees before they are felled. A blacksmith requires more than saplings and scrub.

"These forests won't last forever," said Anton between fierce hammer strikes. "I'll tell ye a secret the Oneidas taught me. Wanting some work done, they brought me this basket of a strange look'ng, darker colored coal. Never seen the like before. The chunks were the color of coffee. Well, this fellow placed a few chunks in the forge for me. I was smelt'ng some iron ore to make this kettle stand, ye see. Oh me, I said, the heat was mighty hot. Do ye know what I did? I said to them, "Dig more of this. It's good!" Anton grinned wide, pointing at the pile of the coffee-colored coal.

More often than serving as Anton's apprentice, Tennent earned his keep with his hunter's trade. He'd leave before dawn and return after dusk, the long, cold hunts. Game was scarce, the absence of hawks indicated this surely enough. Tennent also ranged afar to avoid resentment from the local inhabitants. The region couldn't feed all the people who came to Shamokin. It was safer to avoid scrutiny. His rifle was the best rifle in the region; and he, without boasting, was confident he was the best shot in the region. But it was still the throes of winter, though the promises of spring were beginning to break through. Geese were honking their return. Squirrels began to race about the tree limbs. A robin rooted for a worm.

Then arrived the shad, the celebrated shad time. Tennent had heard the Lenape speak of it. Now, he saw it, with all the joy the river brought. The water ran high and fast. The promise of the Susquehanna invited the people to its waters. They were hungry, and the shad arrived at the time when, after the scarce winter, they were hungriest. After enduring these dismal, distressing months, the miserable inhabitants broke forth as if in a festival, rushing to the river, paddling out in their clumsy dugouts, clustering along the shore with mesh nets. Frantic young boys, who had fashioned tined spears from branches, gathered greedily along the shoreline, even wading out among the rocks. Shad time. The dreary village had become a festival. Kettles shared by families boiled the guts, heads, and skins of the shad. The villagers left nothing for the crows to fight over. Filets of shad stretched out on drying racks. The women sang.

Too many of the men drank. They drank too much. Tennent, wanting to share in the joy of the village, was shoved from behind. The men walked by, insolence on their breath. Heartache rather than defiance filled his soul. He remembered his mother once saying under her breath, during church one Sunday, intending for no one to hear her: "Unless you have wept for others, you never have truly wept."

While the women sang, he stood there suddenly weeping. He was so tired, so weary, so sad for them. Tears streamed across his cheek. He smeared them with the back of his hand. He sniffled and wiped his nose with his neckerchief.

A young girl stood looking at him, wearing a plain buckskin shift. She didn't speak. She didn't have to. Tennent wiped his eyes and smiled at her. Then he exhaled heavily, and more tears came. Palming his face, he laughed at how silly he must appear. Unexpectedly, she reached out to hold his hand. "I like you," she said simply in Susquehannock.

Tennent collected himself, unmindful of the commotion surrounding them. "Well, thank you," he replied in her language, taking her small hand into his.

She smiled. "I like you," she said again, openly, frankly.

"You seem nice yourself." Tennent looked around. "Is your father here?"

"No," she said plainly, "my father left before winter. He has not returned yet."

"And your mother?"

"She is with the women along the shore, gathering the fish for us to eat. My little brother is helping her. They call him, Achgiguwen, the Noisy One, because he is."

"It is a good gathering. It is a time for the people to be happy."

She paused and tightened her hold on his hand. "Why then do you cry?"

Tennent didn't know how to reply. He was unaccustomed to dealing with the forthright innocence of a child. Following her example, he opted for innocence rather than cleverness. "Because I am sad. And because I am glad. I am glad your people will have food to eat. I am sad because, well, my heart breaks when people don't have enough to make themselves happy."

She looked into his face. "You must cry many times then."

He smiled his melancholic smile at her. "Yes, I do, though usually people do not see me do it, unless they are young girls."

It was her turn to smile. "I like you," she said for the third time. "My name is Gagiwanantpehellan."

"I know what that means. It means The Giddy One, right? What a bonny name."

"Like you, you who are known among us as the Man with Two Tomahawks, when I am not crying, I find myself laughing just because I like to laugh. My people think me silly. They do not understand."

Tennent knelt. "That, I understand too well, Giddy One. So, I am glad we are friends, I am glad finally to have a friend." He winked at her playfully.

"Strange," she said looking intently at him, "your eyes are brown, but they seem like the eyes of a cat."

CHAPTER EIGHT

1751

The Susquehannock lass and Tennent did become friends. On the hunt, if he bagged two rabbits, one would go to her mother to help feed Gagiwanantpehellan and her brother; the other he shared with Anton and Catharina. He relished having purpose again. Tennent meant well, yet intention seasoned with kind affection clouded his skill at reading his surroundings. Each hunting success heated the embers of the village's jealousy. He was, after all, an outsider, he was a white man, and he possessed a very fine rifle.

A mid-May snowfall surprised them all one morning. Limbs cracked and fell, especially from the ash trees, the leaves heavy from the moisture. The snow came, the snow melted. Paths were slippery. Sister and Brother went down along the banks of the Susquehanna. Tennent sat on a rock and watched them as he tightened his rifle's flint. An ibis, with its beak resembling a curved blade, and a cormorant, waded upstream. Sister slid to the water's edge in the mud, muckraking, turning over rocks, searching for crawfish and mussel. Brother, armed with a pronged stick he had fashioned, hunted for eels.

"Giddy One," Tennent called out mischievously to her, "Please tell me one thing, because I cannot find anyone to give me the same answer twice. Shamokin, the name, what does it mean? I've been told it is the Place of the Chief. I've been told it is the Place of Crawfish. I've also been told it is the Place of Eels. Which is it?"

The Giddy One giggled, holding her hand to her mouth. "I confess, I also do not know. Maybe we should let the water tell us. Maybe we can choose the name we like best."

Splash! slipped her brother, sliding off the slanted, smooth stone into the river, plunging into the swift spring current. The boy sputtered and yelled, frantic, helpless. They were people of the Susquehanna but very few had ever learned to swim.

Tennent leapt from his rock into the pool below and caught the child before the chilly current swept him downstream. He lifted him and carried him to the shore. The dripping boy hugged his sister.

"Thank you," she said, her gratitude tinged with pleading. "I said you have eyes like a cat. You watch us like a lynx, and you protect us the way a lynx will protect her kittens."

Tennent said, "It's shallow, but these currents can be wickedly deceptive." He reached down and hugged them both. "You're okay now, little sparrows." He held her shaking brother by both shoulders, looking into his face to reassure him. "Noisy One, you must be careful around all water, whether lakes or rivers." Brother looked back at him, scared but curious, wet and trembling, but respectful.

"Haven't you heard about the underwater panther?" Tennent's eyes widened as if alarmed. His hands swept in wide arcs. "Oh yes, wherever you find water you find this monster. He lurks along the bottom of rivers and lakes. Half of his body is a panther, the other half looks like the shell of a snapping turtle, with a long reptile tail that can grab young boys. Sometimes, the water panther grow antlers. Whenever you see the water swirling in a whirlpool, they are near." The boy shivered. "You can hear them growling and hissing like snakes, especially when the winds whirl, the rain is loud, and thunder booms and echoes from the sky. That is why every now and then, when someone falls into the river and he cannot be rescued, the body cannot be found. So, we must always be very careful. We must respect the river the same way we would respect a panther or bear or mountain lion."

None of the three along the bank saw the two men above watching them. These men followed as Tennent escorted Sister and Brother back toward their wigwam to get warm. Gagiwanantpehellan carried her basket containing several mussels. Achgiguwen carried his spear, resolved that next time he'd bring home an eel for supper.

The two men stepped in front of them and blocked the doorway. Gagiwanantpehellan tried to ignore them and push in between. They shoved her back and she fell, the basket rolling in the dirt. Brother attempted to defend her, but he too was shoved aside, one of the men taking his eel spear and breaking it in half. They laughed. Sister and Brother scowled at them.

The two men weren't interested in the children, they were interested in Tennent. He watched them. He waited, holding his rifle by both hands. One of the men reached out for the rifle, going so far as to grab it by the barrel. Tennent ignored him, neither did he allow him to tug it away. Sister and Brother, both embarrassed and angry, stood beside Tennent and faced the two men. The other man suddenly reached for Gagiwanantpehellan and pulled her to him by her arm. She struggled, but his hold on her was too tight. He leaned toward her and sniffed her hair. Tennent waited.

The man restraining Gagiwanantpehellan spoke in Oneida, "You, white man, you like this Susquehannock young girl? We all see how you favor her. Yes? We can give her to you while she still is a flower. She is of our village, our people." Gagiwanantpehellan reddened in a deeper shade of shame and anger. Her brother reached for her, but Tennent stepped in front of him. The man's friend still gripped Tennent's rifle barrel.

Tennent spoke. "She is not yours to give or to take. She is not mine. She is my friend."

The man smiled menacingly, "If you wish to keep your friend safe, we can make a simple trade." Tennent waited. Studying them, he finally recognized them. "We tried to trade with you last week when you had finished one of your hunts," the man said. "Our pelts for your rifle. But you told us to go away and refused to trade with us. You showed us no respect."

"Those pelts were rotten."

"You white men always look down on us. You see, we are poor Oneida. We only hunt with bow and arrow. If we had a great rifle like the rifle of the Man with Two Tomahawks, we could bring back many deer to feed our people. It is a simple thing: this girl for your rifle."

Tennent didn't wait any longer. He knew that the man holding his rifle expected him to try to pull it away. He slammed the barrel forward against the man's face. Cupping his broken nose, the man fell to the ground. With his left hand, Tennent pulled out one of his tomahawks, and swung it toward the other man's forehead, stopping it an inch away. The man's eyes squeezed closed in fear and shame.

Gagiwanantpehellan yanked herself free and hugged her brother.

Quelling his rage, Tennent smiled as he turned the tomahawk horizontally and pressed it against the man's forehead. "Do you know who gave this tomahawk to me? Shikellamy's own son. I warn you, if you or your friend here ever threaten this girl or her family again, not only will the spirit of Shikellamy rise up against you, but his sons also will cast you out, far into the west. Then I personally will hunt you down and leave your carcasses to feed the crows." Tennent sliced the tomahawk sideways to slit the man's forehead till blood seeped. "Do you hear me?"

The man reached down, pulled his friend up, and they stalked off.

* * *

Tennent regretted he hadn't stayed near the river hunting water fowl. Maybe he could have scared up a muskrat or river otter. Instead, he spent the entire frustrating day in the hills, several hills and valleys east of the village, hoping for some pheasants, quail, woodcock, or grouse. He'd be grateful to forage an egg or two.

After a long afternoon, hunting a mile from the river, he finally had discovered several groundhog burrows and waited till twilight for them to venture out from their tunnels. Frog song filled the air. Kneeling perfectly still, he let the first one come fully out before he pulled his trigger. The crack of the rifle chased the other groundhog back into his hole. After bagging the first kill, Tennent waited. The second groundhog stuck out its nose and twitched it before it began to crawl out and over its mound. With daylight fading fast, Tennent didn't wish to wait any longer to fire.

It was the best he could do, only two groundhogs. Fortunately, both were males, so they had a bite or two more meat on them. Gagiwanantpehellan's family would make a feast of them. The fur would make mittens for next winter. *As the poet-preacher wrote, there is a time for killing and a time for healing. Sometimes they are the same.* He swung the bag in front of him. *Killing and healing. Healing and killing. When hasn't life been purchased from death?*

Intent on his kill, his instincts too focused on the food he could bring them, he neglected remaining alert to two-legged predators. Twilight was in his favor; the arrow whisked over him just as he bent to bag the second groundhog. The second arrow struck the ground, missing his foot by an inch. He flattened himself against the ground. He reached for his rifle. He then realized his second mistake. He had placed his rifle on the ground beside the first burrow.

A third arrow swooshed from the tree line. Tennent groaned; a painful groan, followed by a gagging noise, then silence. In the remaining light, two figures emerged from the trees. They hunched over as they crept toward the dark shape lying on the ground. The death groan gave them confidence that their prey lay dead. Still, their training taught them wariness. Kill by ambush. Never take foolish risks.

They crept toward the body, stopped, and listened. There was no gurgle, no breath. One attacker pulled out his knife with his left hand and crept closer. The other held his bow close to his body, an arrow slotted in the string. The man with the bow whispered in Oneida to the other, "My arrow killed him. I claim the rifle."

When the other man turned to argue, Tennent lunged with his knife and plunged it into the back of his nearest attacker's upper thigh. The scout had learned never to back off when attacking, but to always press on, press the advantage. Immediately jumping up, he grasped the wounded man around his neck with his right arm and pulled him in front of his body. His left hand grabbed the man's left wrist to prevent him from using his blade.

The enemy tried to turn Tennent's back toward his companion. Needing to hold his embrace tight, he found he couldn't effectively use his knife or the tomahawks in his belt. He staggered but recovered his footing. He felt the man's left leg giving way. Their cheeks rubbed against each other, and his attacker's paint rubbed off on Tennent's sweaty cheek. The man stank of alcohol. Looking over his enemy's shoulder, he eyed the man's friend armed with the bow and arrow, who tried to circle around to get his shot off. Tennent, mastering the strength of the man he held, kept him between himself and the other. Sensing his opponent weakening, he pressed the man's left arm down, twisted his wrist, and inch by inch pressed the man's own knife below his ribs. He gurgled blood but Tennent held tight and pushed forward to close the distance. Dropping his opponent's knife to the ground, he used both of his arms to shove the dying body toward the man with the bow and arrow. The arrow shot wildly. The man threw down his bow and ran toward the tree line. Tennent dropped to the ground and rolled toward his rifle. He knelt. He paused. He took a breath. He aimed. He took another breath. Exhaling, he fired. Immediately crouching to see beneath the rifle's smoke, he saw the running man stagger and fall forward at the base of an elm, as if prostrating himself before the tree.

Tennent wasn't going to copy their mistake of assuming a kill. Picking up his dropped knife, Tennent twisted it into the throat of the man he had wrestled with. He walked over and did the same to the man he had shot. He sliced the thong of the gourd hanging from that man's neck and poured some its contents onto his bloodied palm. It wasn't water. It was rum. Tennent muttered to himself, "If it had been water, I'd be dead now." He filled his palm and used the rum to wash his opponent's blood from his face, neck, and hands.

He dragged the man he had shot and laid him next to his companion. He looked at them as he reloaded and primed his rifle. The starlight was bright enough for him to see their faces. They were the same two men who tried to trade his rifle for rotten pelts, the two men who threatened his young friends. They were the same two who had threatened Gagiwanantpehellan.

Quickly gutting and bagging the two groundhogs, Tennent exhaled slowly as he listened to the silenced frogs singing again. They sang with the cadence of loose skinned tom-toms, and the cacophony of dozens of squeaky axles and clattering carts, accompanied by their shrill eap, eap, eap, and eager breep, breep, breep, and gargling arup, arup, arup.

Tennent realized that he had to tell Sister and Brother that it was time for him to leave. He must.

CHAPTER NINE

1751

Water cannot help but flow downhill, raindrop to trickle to puddle to ripple to creek to rivulet to stream to river. A river obeys geography, but in so doing shapes geography. Tennent had seen the big rivers, the Hudson, the Delaware. Still, this Susquehanna had done its share of shaping the land.

Susquehanna. The Susquehannocks. Hanna was Algonquin for river. 'Sisawehak' was Lenape for oysters, a staple for the Lenapes who lived at the mouth of the river and its wide bay. The river's water, nutrients, and silt helped form the rich and thick oyster beds and reefs down beyond in the Chesepiooc. Oyster shells were abundant, and clean water. Fresh water merged with salt water. 'Sisa'we'hak'hanna' for 'Oyster River,' or, possibly, from 'assisku' for mud. 'Siskëwahane,' the 'Muddy River,' given how shallow it is. Or, perhaps, 'Crooked River.' Names can be confusing, depending on who is naming the name.

Either way, day and night, these sleepless rivers heave and flow, rivers turn sullen and shallow, rivers overflow banks, rivers carve ruts and canyons, rivers pool and stagnate. Tumid rivers back up the streams and creeks which, unable to flow downhill, swell and spread where tumescent water will. There is no malevolence to the flow or flood of water. Water does what water must, what water will. Tennent smiled at how we brazenly think we can control such passions. Rivers breathe and press, lunge and pulsate, evade and find new paths. A river nods at the works of man but in so doing shapes man. She defines us as us. We drink it, we are fed by it, we gambol in it, we've worked on it, we've been baptized in it, we explore it, we've died in it. Rivers. Rivers mean crops. Rivers mean commerce. Rivers mean industry. Rivers mean towns and cities. Rivers mean community. Rivers mean life.

The two branches of the Susquehanna River, like parted lovers, eventually converge to flow as one. The North Branch, he's been told, is born somewhere upstream in the province of New York. On day, he vowed, I'll make that trek.

She travels steady and strong where she meets the West Branch here at Shamokin, the West Branch fed by the trickle streams and springs near the base of the Tuscaroras as she squiggles north before bending east around the Great Island, then where Otstonwakin once thrived, finally flowing south toward here. Rivers roll on. Upstream affects downstream, every time. And not just in rivers.

A river starts off as mere trickle, widening as other streams feed it, contribute to it, fill it. From bubble to stream to vast river flowing full, it grows and widens and flows. The Susquehanna he's lived near these years reminded a pensive, philosophical Tennent of how our lives become filled and deepened and richer and broader through the years as tributary others we have met have contributed to us, filled us. We are the river. Rivers are us. It is us. We drink it. It feeds us. From gnat to shad to bear to fox to lynx. From mussel to eagle to us.

* * *

"Where will you travel now?" she asked, her eyes also tearing up.

"Upstream, upstream. When in doubt, head upstream," he answered, winking at her with a wet eyelid.

Tennent knelt, reached out, and squeezed his hand on her brother's shoulder. "Noisy One, you shall soon be a Susquehannock brave. A brave, above all things, protects his family. Your mother and sister need you. What I am about to tell you may not sound like the way of a Susque-hannock brave, yet there are times when pride can prevent a man from truly being a man. I've talked with the black-smith. Anton Schmidt is a good man, he said he will find work for you to do, if you are willing to learn a trade."

Tennent's eyes glistened mischievously. "Take this and use it well. Be careful to avoid falling in." He pulled from his haversack the head of trident, with each of the three prongs barbed. "Fashion yourself a good shaft, secure it tight, and there'll be plenty of eel and shad for you to eat. Mr. Schmidt forged it just for you, Achgiguwen."

He reached again into his haversack and pulled out a small item wrapped and tied in leather. "For you, Gagiwa-nantpehellan. I've carried it this with me for several years now, ever since I left my home. This gift belonged to my mother. I want you to have it. She would be pleased that what she loved is finally in good hands."

Gagiwanantpehellan untied the thong and carefully unwound the leather wrapping. She lifted up the pair of embroidery scissors. The Giddy One began to weep freely.

"Enough," he said, rising to kiss her on her forehead. He looked up to the sky and recited a line of poetry from John Donne: "A globe, yea would by that impression grow, Till thy teares mixt with mine doe overflow, This world, by waters sent from thee, my heaven dissolved so." He smiled a wan smile, turned, and headed upstream. Achgiguwen and Gagiwanantpehellan watched him disappear into the woods before they climbed back into their borrowed dugout canoe and paddled their way to their home, the morning sunshine cresting the southern undulating hills and skipping across the rippling waters.

Almost five miles upstream, Tennent spotted the huge nest high in a tree on an island near the southern bank of the river. How long, he wondered, had it been their home? How many eaglets hatched over the years high above this island thick with tall trees? A nest made of enormous sticks, many necessarily thick, plus a bedding of grass and moss, he imagined. He had learned how mated eagles commit to building the nest together, ever trying to improve it. Nesting. The nesting instinct. A quick swoop, talons at the ready, and, presto, a wiggling smallmouth bass for all the hungry eaglets opening their beaks and screeching, cheeping. Looking around, he noticed what might have been a warren for a family of rabbits. Tennent rubbed his scratchy chin and smiled, thinking, I guess my home isn't so much one place, is it?

After waiting to see if an eagle would return to the nest, he decided it was time to press on. The terrain he entered was long, pleasant flatland, edged by a long continuous hill to his left, the Susquehanna off to his right. He felt as if he were entering a place that few visited. He watched the river roll downstream, his heart tinged with a sadness both restless and contented. There was a feel of sanctuary about this place. He wiped his eyes with his sleeve. Oh, my Susquehanna. How much I want to love you. How much I despair over how we have treated you.

Eventually he came to where the hill and the Susque-hanna pressed close to each other. A few signs along the bank indicated small hunting parties had visited here on occasion. There was a campfire, long spent, built between rounded roots, a piece of weathered buckskin fringe snagged by a thorn of a wild raspberry bush. He followed his whims. A small trickling stream at the base of a rugged escarpment intrigued him. The height to the top of the cliff was about the height of a shaded dogwood tree. "That would be nasty fall," he commented to no one. After refilling his gourd with the fresh water, he followed the stream through the compact gorge until he could climb a small rise and backtrack toward the top of the cliff. The outcropping provided for a small open space where Tennent decided to make camp for the night. "If anyone tries to sneak up on me, they have to come one way." Gathering tinder from dry shrubs, he struck the flint from his tinderbox, fed the flame a few sticks. He checked his shot bag and, given the lead ingots he had molded into shot while staying with Anton, he figured he had more than enough. He cleaned his rifle, rinsed the barrel, inspected his moccasins. It was the hunter's routine. Water, corn, and salted eel supplied his supper. He reclined on his haversack, folded his hands behind his head, and looked up. Several bats fluttered by. The open space afforded a window into the eastern night sky. He was fond of the constellation Cygnus, for it suggested a swan's long neck with his wings curved in flight heading east. Orpheus, so the ancient myth described, had been transformed from death into this swan, with his lyre at hand. Tracing the sky with his finger, he traced the other name for Cygnus, the Northern Cross. Still tracing, he formed the great triangle from the three brightest stars. He liked it here.

Come morning, he spotted deer tracks and scat near the stream's edge. The blueberry-looking pellets were still moist and dark and shiny. They had been forest eating, with smaller piles indicating does. He followed them westerly a mile or so, skirting back along the bottom of the rounded hill, which ran along for a distance resembling a rolled-up blanket, soft and rumpled. The doe tracks jumped right, up into the hillside. He followed until he broke through a line of trees and came upon a sight unlike any he had seen before.

This was a field of rocks, covering at least two acres. Unlike the jumbled boulders south of the Alleghene, here time hadn't had a chance to smooth out the rough edges the way time does to sharp rocks and, one hopes, to raw young men alike. Encircled by the woods was a confused debris field of jagged, contorted, ankle-breaking rocks. Jagged and jutted, rough and ragged, this seemed like a field of frag-ments of tombstone rubbish. Did furious giants chip-knap their fearsome spears here? Or is this a place where the devil himself might bed down for the night? *Father used to quote in his sermons,* joked Tennent silently, *how you'll never get to heaven on a featherbed.*

Hearing several rattles sound from crevices in the rocks, Tennent avoided crossing over them, and instead hiked around the debris field. *If the devil isn't sleeping here, rattlers sure are. Thank you for warning me. Some things really are best left alone. Can't blame rattlesnake if you get bit. The real deviltry isn't the rocks or the rattlers but from those who fail to respect, poking around where they don't belong. At least the rattlesnakes warn you, unlike many men.* Tennent smirked at his soliloquy.

Leaning forward due to the steep grade, at times clawing the ground or grabbing saplings, often finding it easier to tack diagonally, Tennent moved uphill, away from the bizarre rocks. Resting, he noticed one spindly mountain laurel rising from the slope. It appeared straggly, but this orphan nonetheless impressed him. Mountain laurel, he knew, grew into thick shrubs. There seemed in this laurel a will to live. What gave it its yearning, its insistent force to live, to grow, to flourish, to be? For some reason Tennant wished he could tell his father that there may be one Word of God, but there also is the testament of nature. Yes, the Bible gives revelation, but nature speaks also. Why do we differentiate between sacred and profane, when it is all sacred?

This mountain laurel that Tennent admired suggested something far more than a pretty shrub, so straggly and solitary and defiant as the laurel sought sunlight. Defiance—that was what attracted Tennent to it. It refused to be stunted by the shade trees surrounding it. Tennent looked up through the leaves and shielded his eyes.

Roots sinking deep and wide, grabbing hold of dirt, minerals, water and consuming all it can. Leaves opening and beckoning the sunlight. This energy of light absorbed; this energy of sunlight transformed into green life. Life increasing life. It reaches for life. He leaned toward it, believing he could hear this solitary mountain laurel breathe. The laurel also was clever enough to lean upon a neighbor tree to support its spindly trunk as it reached toward the sun.

He liked it here, even when he nearly stumbled into a momma black bear and her cubs. He could have blamed himself for his folly. Instead, mockingly, he blamed the bees. He heard the thrumming, saw a bee, and bee-lined rashly toward the thrumming. There he saw the bees clustered, swarming and buzzing at an opening in a tree. Eagerly, he rummaged through his haversack for his stubby stone pipe, tobacco, and tinderbox. He began to shred the tobacco and stuff the clay bowl. There would be the double pleasure of a smoke, and smoking out the bees. Given the shadows of the forest, and his sweet tooth, he failed to see momma bear. She growled confidently. Tennent backed off obediently. With a courteous wave, he said, "All yours, madam. Please do enjoy." Then he retreated away far enough to avoid being blamed by angry bees, while momma bear started clawing away at the bark. He watched. He waited for his turn.

Licking his fingers from remnants of honeycomb, he let the wistful contours of the smooth and worn hills lead him. He liked it here. These were old hills, mature hills. Time had gentled them. This was another issue over which he had disagreed with his father. The earth could not be as young as some Biblical scholars calculated. He breathed deep the smell of dirt. This could only be the work of eons.

Kneeling, he reached down and scooped up a handful of dirt. Opening his fingers, he let the dirt fall back to the ground. "What a gift," he said aloud to himself. "What are trees but expressions of earth herself? What a variety." He was surrounded by an abundant, virgin forest—elm, hemlock, ash, fir, sassafras, sumac, spruce, oak, dogwood, hickory, beech, sugar maple. "You might just suppose

God is sending us message in the variety. Nature seeks balance. Nature creates diversity. Diversity brings bounty and beauty. Even the dirt and rocks proclaim this gospel of diversity and difference."

Sandstone, limestone, granite, quartz, shale. The rocks, especially those fresh from rockslide, displayed their colored striations: shades of brown and gray, tinges of green and blue. Many were, like the Lenape warrior, painted in black and red.

"Who are those naïve poets," he scoffed, "who romanticize being bathed in the stillness and silence of the forest. Come, friend, and learn of your mistake. Listen to how beautifully loud is the music, when you have ears to hear. Whirr and buzz, croak and caw, rustling wind, it's all motion. It's all a conversation, stories told."

A swallow twittered by, as if mocking him. Tennent called after him, "Do remember, I am a preacher's son. Let those who have ears to hear . . ."

With the sun now at his back, he found himself drifting downhill. The higher part of the hill opposite him still received the sunlight, turning the green leaves into the color of lemon. Off to the right, through the trees, he could look back and see where the Susquehanna curved toward the southwest. It seemed natural to him that once he reached the valley, he'd come across a creek. Raspberry tea would not be amiss, he fancied, glancing about for some raspberry bushes. At the base of the slope, he came across both creek and raspberries. Brook trout idled in the water, periodically waving their tails against the flow. He dandled his fingers at the hovering dragonfly which disappeared in a flaming flicker. The splash of his hook scattered the trout and water

skeeters, but only momentarily. Two little trout he released
back into the creek. A larger one he kept. There he camped,
ate, and relaxed. He admired the nearby patch of wild thistles. He was fond of thistles: beautiful, thorny, deep rooted.
The setting was so tranquil that he had to remind himself
to tend to his rifle. With furrowed eyebrows, he chastised
himself, for he was becoming careless.

The next morning proved to him that caution wasn't
undue. Following the creek as it meandered toward the
Susquehanna, he came to a recent campsite at its mouth.
Moccasin prints remained readable. A circle of stones indicated a commonly used campfire. Under a shrub he found a
midden of mussel shells and frog bones. Smacking his lips,
he had a sudden hankering for frog legs. He'd have to make
a gig. A few temporary shelters were scattered at the edge of
the clearing, hinting at regular usage. This seemed like an
ideal spot for a hunting party to visit. Possibly, it could have
been a site desired for a longer stay. A few fragments of clay
pots and chips of stone for shaping arrowheads suggested
as much. The wrecked eel weir in the creek told the same
story. He pictured several families arriving here—whether
Oneida or Lenape, or Shawnee—and enjoying its gifts.

Two hawks circled above as he dipped his neckerchief
into the river, twisted it, and washed his face and neck. The
water dribbled down the back of his shirt. A kingfisher rat-
tled and klecked, eager to pounce on a perch. A great blue
heron, with its S-shaped neck, strode elegantly along the
bank, half hidden by tree limbs bent and dipping into the
water. He liked it here. The river, the creek, the woods—an
ideal place to rest and feel content. The midden inspired
him to search for his own mussels along the water's edge.

If he had a kettle he would have boiled them. Instead, he heated those he gathered inside the circle of rocks, sprinkling them until they opened. Two dozen shells added to the pile. He, too, left his mark for others to find.

A mallard taking flight in its comically frantic paddle and flap drew his attention downstream. The ripples, which he had assumed were caused by the duck, suggested something else. He spotted a larger, and evidently permanent, weir under the water where the mallard flew off. With the water low, the familiar V-riffles of flowing water indicated a V formation of rocks on the river bottom. When you bother to look, the current reveals. Somebody placed those stones there. Obviously intentional. Who? When? How long have other people come here and taken advantage of this gift that others built before?

He liked it here.

CHAPTER TEN

1800

The decanter sat empty on the lowboy. The Bracket clock chimed. There was yet an hour 'til the time when Hannah said she would serve the simple evening supper—leftover chicken pieces, plus porridge in the Dutch oven. The two old men dozed peacefully. A clay pipe lay across Montgomery's lap. Ruth slept curled at Tennent's feet, her head resting on her paws. The sun poured through the room's window, the beam of sunlight slowly drifting from the back of the bench toward the painting on the wall.

The men blinked and rubbed their eyes when they heard the front door creaking open.

"Hello," a young man announced as he stepped over the threshold and crossed under the lintel. "Father, we're here."

A woman's voice sang out from the end of the hallway. "Come, come, Daniel, Alexander. Welcome. They're in the sitting room, where they've run out of both whiskey and stories."

Colonel Montgomery leaned toward Tennent. "Third wives have an annoying tendency to speak too candidly. God love my Hannah."

Tennent smiled and stood up to greet the two young men who entered the room. Ruth swished her tail. The elder of the two was dressed more formally than the younger, wearing the traditional buttoned waistcoat with large pockets, and a green frock coat, his stockings tied below his knees with ribbons, his dark hair tied back. The younger, having come from the fields, arrived with the sleeves of his linen shift rolled up, his breeches tucked into his riding boots, his hair hanging loose.

"Two of my boys, Tennent. You've met my older boy, Daniel, several times before. He's become a man of distinction and position."

"Yes, I can see. I recall. You, Daniel, were a pup the first time we met. That first time was a long time ago, at Fort Augusta with your mother, Isabella, God rest her soul."

"Yes, sir. We miss her."

"Some dark days, back in '78. Tallow days. You, I remember, were twelve years old, and despite the threat, not scared a stitch. You wanted to rush back with your father and defend the farm with your brothers. You must now be, what, thirty-five years old."

Daniel shuffled sheepishly before he looked up at Tennent. "I have a confession, sir, which has bothered me for years. At Augusta, you gave me something very special. Your tomahawk. The one with the iron inlays.

"Ah yes, Shikellamy's own son gave that to me."

"Which makes my confession worse, I fear. Several years after you trusted me with it, I was horsing around one day with my older brothers. Showing off, I suppose. I thought I could hit this tree, you see." Daniel coughed. "I missed the tree and threw the tomahawk into the Susquehanna. I waded in to try to find it but couldn't."

Tennent applauded with delight. "Ah, so you didn't bury the hatchet, you drowned it. We should have done that long ago with all the tomahawks. Good for you, you discovered the secret to peace."

"All is forgiven. The past is past," said the Colonel. "Thanks be to God." Montgomery squeezed his hand on

Daniel's shoulder. "Well married, Daniel is, with their fifth child on the way."

"Fine, fine. Good for you. I always wondered what it would be like," Tennent said wistfully. "And this young man must be . . . ?"

"Alexander the Fourth," Daniel announced, slapping his brother on the arm.

Tennent narrowed his brow in confusion. "I'm confused."

"I'm the fourth in the Montgomery family to bear this name, our grandfather's name," said Alexander. "Although, I didn't discover this until I was at an age willing to listen and learn. Two older brothers, each named Alexander, failed to survive infancy."

"My dear Margaret Mary, my first wife, suffered much grief as a mother in her day," explained the Colonel. "It's ironic, I suppose," reflected William Montgomery, "how new birth involves moaning and pain. Only our three boys, out of the seven children she birthed, still survive."

"That was well before father relocated here from the farm in Chester County," continued Alexander after a respectful pause. "Father always wanted to name one son after his father, the original Alexander. I've been privileged to receive this legacy. Along with the responsibility," he added with youthful pride.

Tennent shook the young man's hand. "Few know this, but my given name is the same as yours. It is a burden we Alexanders share, especially when you know your Greek."

"It is my turn to be confused," confessed Alexander.

"I mean the meaning of the name. Ah, you're still adrift. Let me explain. It was important to my own family that the name you bore would become manifested in your character. A family conceit, if you will. Margaret, for example, comes from old Hebrew in the Bible, meaning Pearl. A pearl of great price. The pearl to the Hebrews symbolized the Word of God. The name of your father's current wife, Hannah, also from Scripture, aptly means From Grace."

Tennent placed his hand on the Colonel's back. "William, which is of course your father's name, means Determined Protector. A warrior's name. Will-helm; helm, as in a helmet. It fits your father, doesn't it? Your sister did say he does look grand on a horse."

William shook his head and waved Tennent away. "Ah yes, the great and gallant warrior who had to be tumbled into the dirt by a scrofulous scout to avoid being decapitated by a cannon ball."

Tennent continued. "Daniel here—a name also from the Bible, such as faithful Daniel who was tested in the lion's den, though perhaps now it is a den filled with fellow men of commerce and trade—is pronounced in Hebrew, Dan-i-el, meaning, God has judged. El in Hebrew means God, Lord."

"And Alexander? My name. Excuse me, sir. Our name."

"From the Greek, Alexandros. The Latin form is alexo, meaning I defend, and andros, meaning man. Defender of Man. Since the Revolution, I prefer to translate it as Defender of We the People."

Tennent slapped his thigh and guffawed loudly, startling all three Montgomery men. "Your father is prone to giving speeches. When I get talking, I'm prone toward the pedantic, like my professorial pastoral family. The result, I fear, of spending too much taciturn time in the woods by myself, with only Ruth here to keep me company these days." At her name being mentioned, the dog perked up, expecting a treat. "There have been times, I admit, when I gravely missed community, and intelligent, congenial conversation. When I venture into towns, I seem to lose my forest habits. My only cure is to return to the trees."

"I never knew that is what my name meant. Professor Tennent, I have a nut for you to crack. What about the name Jane?

The Colonel wagged his finger at his son Alexander to explain. "Jane is the name of the young woman he fancies."

"Ah," rejoined Tennent. "That is a puzzler. I'll have to think on that one. Could be an abbreviation, I suppose. Or the feminine form of the name John. Or is that Joan? It, nevertheless, is an old name." He placed his hand on Alexander's shoulder. "Since it is the name of the girl you fancy, I suppose you best should discover what the name means. What it means to you is far more important."

"Since we are playing parlor games with names, Tennent," said the Colonel, "tell my boys your Indian name."

"Colonel, I've just about used up my allotment of words for one day."

"Please, sir," entreated Daniel. "Father can only allude to your adventures, and . . . well, we've had so few adventures of our own."

Alexander finished his brother's thought, knowing full well his brother's mind. "We're farmers and merchants. The wildest adventures we've ever experienced have been those two occasions when we visited Philadelphia, especially that time we visited Dr. Franklin."

"Never have met that great man, though I certainly have heard stories about him," offered Tennent.

Alexander began speaking excitedly. "Daniel at least can remember the Big Runaway and Fort Augusta. Me? I was a mewling infant then. Nowadays, the only Indians we see are the few poor souls who visit our Trading Post." He glanced over his shoulder. "Is that your rifle in the hall-way? Looks like a handsome piece. I noticed it is one of the newer Lancaster models with both a set trigger and a hair-trigger for accuracy."

"Watch out for this one, Colonel, he sounds like me over fifty years ago when I left college for this frontier."

"Farming and shop keeping is adventure enough. Enterprise and industry and creating a way of life is adventure enough," advised William Montgomery.

"Oh, Father, we meant no disrespect. By the way, Daniel told me Uncle Daniel intends to stop by after supper."

"Alas, the good General's rye seems to have disappeared while we slept away the afternoon. Your uncle shall go parched."

Alexander looked around at the glasses.

"Washington's first name is George," said Tennent ruefully. "Now there's a fitting name for a farmer, don't you think, Alexander?" asked Tennent. "From the Greek 'georgos,' meaning tiller of the soil, of the earth, 'geo.' Dirt, as your father here would remind you, is indeed honorable and precious. I only wish the good General had been given by our Lord more years to enjoy his farm. How many men would have refused a third term? Instead, he walked away from power." He turned toward Montgomery. "Would Adams?"

The Colonel pounded his fist into his left hand. "If we Democratic Republicans have our way, that Federalist won't get reelected President to get the chance to decide. We'll have our day when Jefferson takes office."

Tennant communed with his own political thoughts. Tick, tock, goes the clock. The gears crank from the swing of the pendulum, right then left, left to right, back and forth, proving that our feverish windings haven't broken the clock. Yet. Tennent smiled to himself. Whatever happened to the pursuit of the common good, of common sense?

Colonel Montgomery handed the decanter to Alexander. "Perhaps, son, you could find another jug out back for us all to share a toast later?"

"Gladly, father." Alexander beamed. "I'll go ask your wife where she's hidden your secret cache." Alexander gestured toward Tennent. "Might I first hear how Mr. Tennent received his Indian name?"

"Son, we will wait for your return."

"Leni Lenape, to be precise," Tennent clarified. "My Delaware name. My name given from The Unami. The First People. Those before all others. The telling will require a shared sip. To understand the name, I'll have to take you back to the day when I first met our venerable Cincinnatus, when President Washington was a mere captain."

"I'll be right back," said Alexander eagerly.

CHAPTER ELEVEN

1755

The tall captain moved at sunrise among the panicked men awakening from the darkest night of the month, calmly organizing the remnants of Braddock's command. Worry had escalated into alarm. Alarm had essayed into panic. All that the captain knew for certain was that Braddock, though mortally wounded, had ordered a full retreat back to Fort Cumberland along same the road they had labored months constructing, and that Dunbar's reserve force with the baggage train remained intact.

"Tennent." The captain addressed him softly, calmly. "Please be kind enough to find Lieutenant Fraser and tell him to have you and your scouts protect the rear guard. Do not, I repeat; do not, have him include his Mingos. The men are scared enough to shoot even our few friendlies."

"So, Captain," Tennent smirked quietly as he tightened the jaw screw to his flint and tested the frizzen. "You want us to be the rear guard to the rear guard?" He opened the frizzen and blew into the pan and touch hole.

"You assess my intentions correctly. I don't need blue jays raiding my nest."

"At your service. One thing, Captain, would you be so kind as to remind the rear guard that we friendlies be skulking about the woods also, so it's not just the hostiles. Make sure they know how a turkey gobbles—we'll do that when we want to let them know not to shoot at us. Not that they could hit a damn thing."

"At your service, Mr. Tennent." The officer smiled broadly. "Tell Fraser also that Dunbar intends to destroy our cannon and burn all the wagons—we can't slow down the retreat." His countenance betrayed his true mood. "What a bloody mess. What a disaster. We're only provincials, why should they bother listening to us?" he asked sarcastically. "Pray, Tennant, that the French are too surprised by their victory along this Menaonkihela River that they won't want to pursue us. Nor do we need the Shawnee and Delaware eager for more scalps. The scent of blood is intoxicating. Thank God, Shingas and his bunch of Delawares stayed out of it, for now. Damn those French for persuading them to fight for them to get their land back, bribing them with promises they never intend to keep. When the British lie, they know they are lying. When the French lie, they believe it as gospel truth, for the moment."

"Not that our own incursions into their lands didn't incite them to fight us," Tennent observed dryly.

The Captain wiped his brow with his sleeve. "What a bloody mess."

"That it is, that it is. How many of us are left?"

Washington simply shook his head. "Good luck, scout. Keep me posted." Captain Washington watched with sorrow as his scout vanished into the deep woods. He felt sorry for his scouts. Their battles always were solitary battles. Sometimes ambushed, they would never return, their fate hidden, unmarked, unknown, undiscovered. But their fate could be guessed at, for it wouldn't have been the French who could ambush them. Their fate? Likely it would be similar to the fate of the twelve captured British soldiers tied to stakes in front of Fort Duquesne, tortured, scalped alive, burnt alive.

How could those young men who enlisted from Cornwall or Devonshire or York have imagined frontier warfare?

Their training was to stand in line, load muskets three times a minute, present arms, fire at the opposing line, then charge with bayonet. The colonials understood frontier warfare because they suffered it and because they practiced it, sometimes with a madness worse and more ruthless than the Shawnee or Delaware or Tuscarora or Mohawk. This was war for no gentleman officer. This was Old Testament horror. Women kidnapped to become slaves. If not made captives, then stripped and scalped, their babies smashed against trees.

"Good luck, scout," he said again, this time to the wind.

Having informed Lieutenant Fraser of the Captain's orders, Tennent gathered ten of the remaining fellow scouts, those who either survived or hadn't drifted off. Together, they agreed to the territory each would cover. Fraser remained with the rear guard to receive any news the scout might discover of the enemy's proximity. Two of the younger scouts he kept as runners.

Nodding to each other, the scouts, some dressed Lenape style in buckskin leggings and the one-piece breechclout, shod in moccasins, filtered into the forest with a stealth to match their enemies.

* * *

The bullet burnt the skin of his forearm. The shot was followed by the familiar whoop. Tennent turned to meet his attacker. His aim off his hip was deadlier. A second Delaware rushed at him through the smoke with raised tomahawk. Flipping his rifle in his hands, he slammed the butt of the rifle into the face of the warrior, stunning him insensate, bloodying him. He spied the movement of what he hoped was only one more enemy. Tennent turned to run. Gunfire crackled. A bullet passed through his hunting frock. Dashing from tree to tree, he reloaded his rifle. Finding cover, he searched in vain for his pursuer. Like a doe hiding secluded in a thicket, he waited. No sounds came from the woods. He waited a little longer, his nostrils dilated, listening to his own heartbeat, listening for the tick of a gunlock. He waited until the birdsong returned. A squirrel raced about a tree trunk, climbed to the first limb, and chirped at him for this intrusion. Tennent was assured his last attacker had abandoned the fight. The scout retraced his flight and returned to where the fight began. The two bodies remained. Tennant cradled his rifle, saying to himself, *Must be stragglers. No true Delaware or Shawnee warrior would abandon these braves like this. Well, white or red, we all have our maggots.*

Just before sunset turned into night, Tennent passed through the spiked cannons that had been abandoned and what was left of the blackened wagons, and returned to Fraser and the Rear Guard, which had already marched miles southeast down Braddock's Road, away from the failed battle. Braddock's defeat. Braddock's retreat. Tennent's observations agreed with the reports of his fellow scouts. The French weren't in pursuit and the Delawares were distracted by the frenzy of scalping over five hundred dead soldiers left behind.

CHAPTER TWELVE

1800

Tennant took a long, slow, tired drink of rye. The eyes of the two young men were transfixed on him.

Warfare disgusted Tennent, which is why warfare became his profession. War had a way of tracking him down. All he really wanted to do was explore, and hunt when he needed to eat or clothe himself. After Alexander had returned with the full decanter, glasses filled, Tennent simply smelled the rye and spun it around in his glass, watching the legs of the whiskey slide back down. In his core, raised in faith and reverence, raised to depend upon a daily dose of repentance and forgiveness, he hoped he could demonstrate a kernel of morality in the most immoral of human conditions. In his heart he wanted to protect others, to defend those who needed to be defended. He fought for who needed him to fight. It wasn't in his nature to fight for what others wanted him to fight for.

Nature, he had learned from his college of the forest, seeks balance, even when it may seem brutal and harsh. Brutality is an interpretation, an attribution given it by conscientious sentiments, indeed, by those of us given consciousness, awareness. Tennent rubbed Ruth's neck with the toe of his boot. Does my Ruth really know she is a dog? Nature may be harsh, but is it really brutal? Nature is morally indifferent. We paste onto nature, Tennent believed, what we think about ourselves. Nature is nature, unlike human nature. Human nature has a choice.

A snake sinking fangs in you isn't from malice aforethought, no more than those mosquitoes biting you or a wasp stinging. It just is. It just is their Nature. Never seen an eagle torment a fish just to torment it. Never seen those mountain lions prowling about the Nit-a-nees kill or torture out of pure, gratuitous spite. Nothing mean about it. They kill when they are hungry or when their young'ns are hungry. Neither righteous nor evil, just is. It's their instinct, their nature. We're supposed to be rational. It's not as if those honest predators choose to kill or torment, unlike us human predators. The good Lord help us, we enjoy it. We justify it.

He spoke over the lip of the glass. "I'm grateful to say, men, I've always tried to avoid starting a fight. I've never been proud of killing a man when I felt I had no choice, nor am I ashamed when the deed was required. There's more to being a man than anger and vengeance. We're intended to be better than our natures." Tennent took another sip. "I have watched and learned from the bear, the wolves, the mountain lions. Do you know which among the beasts rules the others? Never the one who snarls the fiercest or intimidates the others. The sharpest teeth or snarl isn't what secures dominance. The wolf runs in family units, mom and dad raising pups. Discipline among the pack happens because it is encouraged through the true strength of needing each other. Not sure that's a choice either. Still, we humans could learn from them. I've never seen an animal kill for spite or pleasure."

The young men waited.

"After we straggled back to Fort Cumberland, hungry, tired, spent, we were informed that Captain Washington and the various militias under his command were assigned to protect the entire frontier. Dunbar, however, didn't wait around. He kept retreating until he reached the comforts of Philadelphia. We colonials, we provincials, were on our own. And the French and Delawares had us on our heels." Tennent rubbed his forehead gravely, then clutched his hands together. "Colonel, it never occurred to me till now, telling this tale. What do you think? That defeat might have been the moment when we began to doubt the British, believing that we Americans could do better without them. Hmmm, interesting. Never thought of that."

"Is that when you received your Delaware name?" Daniel asked, also taking a sip.

The Colonel answered instead, "No, my boys. Be patient. Our scout here is setting the table for the worse yet to come. Not only is the scent of blood intoxicating, so is the stench of vengeance. While all this deviltry took place west of Delaware, where I grew up, I was a mere lad preoccupied with a lad's distractions, an orphan still years shy of my majority. My brother and sisters had to rely on each other till we went our ways. We also had the blessing of being active in our White Clay Creek Presbyterian Church where our guardians worshipped and took care of us. I turned twenty-one in 1757—that's when I was able to settle on your grandfather's Londonderry property. God's providence guided me as I tried to learn how to turn our family's land into a productive farm."

"You, Colonel, were, what then? Twenty years old when the Braddock Defeat took place—July 1755," continued Tennent. "I spent the next months tracking raiding parties from the Alleghene to the Susquehanna, even as far south as the Patowmac, trying to keep the authorities abreast of the threats. Tracking along all the different paths, trails.

Remember, by treaty, our beautiful Susquehanna marked the frontier, the boundary-line. Remember also, with the wave of European settlers arriving here, we ignored the boundaries."

Interrupting, the Colonel added, "How do you bring into cooperation two different cultures? Daniel, what are you and your uncle busy doing now? Surveying the land. It is what I did. We survey land. We mark it off. We sell it. We own land."

Tennent nodded. "Lenape, Oneida, all—they claim territory, but don't own it. Which is why the tribes migrated toward the Ohi-yo and Great Lakes, along with all the bitter resentment that went with their forced exodus. With Braddock's defeat, and French encouragement, the tribes sought to return to their lands here. Violent raids increased. This Susquehanna frontier was judged vulnerable. It was. Then in October, five days before the Hunter Moon, the massacre at the Kaarondinhah—what you now call Penn's Creek—took place. You probably know the place where it happened, it's only twenty miles downstream from here. What do you call the place now? Yes, Selin's Grove. Although, I seem to recall the settlers first referred to it as Weisertown, after my old acquaintance. Ah, names, names, names. To remind you, young men, all this was new territory to us. You Montgomerys hadn't arrived yet. Serving Washington then, I was two years older than you, Alexander, are now."

"The massacre was done by the Delawares, wasn't it?" asked Daniel.

"Everything is complicated." Tennent snapped his fingers, startling Ruth. "Have you played the game Jack-Straws? You pull out one straw and try to prevent the others from moving, right? Nearly impossible. I spent my first year on the frontier visiting and living among the Leni Lenape and a remnant of the Susquehannocks—I grew to admire them, respect them, even loved several of them as good and trustworthy friends. It helps to appreciate how the Iroquois Confederacy and the Leni Lenape were frequently in contention with each other. The Leni felt the Iroquois cheated them. And they did. This whole valley once was their land, having come here from the south and from along the Delaware River after having lost their rights to the land there. Of course, the Susquehannocks got overwhelmed by them. But the Iroquois, willfully corrupted by unscrupulous politicians . . ."

"By Jove! How dare you, old friend, imply we magistrates could be unscrupulous," teased Montgomery with feigned umbrage.

Tennent hummed before continuing, ". . . hmmm, yes . . . and sold the land on the west side of the Susquehanna to the provincial government, who in turn sold it to new settlers. The Leni Lenape kept getting pushed farther west. How would you respond?"

"I'd plead my case in court," replied Daniel.

"That's because you trust the courts. What if you didn't? Which courts? Either way, with the French successes westward some segments of the Shawnee and Leni Lenape population listened to the warriors among them, rallying them to reclaim their lands. They felt license to seek revenge. Not all, but some did, the young braves especially, compelled by the desire to prove their manhood."

"Human nature evinced once again," commented the Colonel. "Depravity comes too easy. Once again, regardless our skin, we are driven more by spleen than by mind or heart, less by the restraining grace and goodness of God."

"Jack straws, boys. This time including rum. Wanting to prove their manhood, those Lenape braves attacked the settlers along the Penn's Creek. Sometimes it seemed the Susquehanna flowed with more rum than water. Then with blood. It was again a time of rifles, tomahawks, and knives. Cabins and fields were set afire. Men were slaughtered in ambush, along with women and children. Scalps were taken. Fourteen settlers were murdered at your Penn's Creek. The surviving women and children were taken as captives." Tennent slumped back on his bench. "So, good fellows, what comes next?"

"Justice," decreed Daniel.

"Revenge," guessed Alexander.

"Some say Justice means simply to be able to hunt in your own woods and eat your porridge in peace. I've never figured out how Justice can be synonymous with that Latin term, *Lex Talionis*. That stern law, I admit, is the Lenape way. The law of retribution. I confess, that it also is often enough our tribe's way too. We've forgotten that when our Bible prescribed an eye for eye, it proscribed wanton vengeance, that this was a moral improvement suppressing feuds and mitigating the slaughter of your enemy's entire family. And eye for an eye tried to establish some frame of law to fence our unholy passions. Eye for an eye. Tooth for tooth. Hand for hand. Foot for foot. Life for life. See what results when we keep stirring this cauldron of hate? We unleash the demons. That's the problem, and the sickness. It's our brew. Well, fellows, word spread downriver of the massacre. John Harris, who

I met five years before at the very beginning of what you gentlemen refer to as my adventures, rallied his neighbors; soon four dozen armed men marched their way north toward Shamokin Village."

"*Lex Talionis*," said Alexander.

"Rumors had circulated that the raid at Penn's Creek was staged by braves from Shamokin. Harris wanted to make sure another raid wouldn't happen again. Shamokin was then still an important Indian center, where you now call by the English name, Sunbury. Just before Harris' expedition reached Shamokin, a man of mixed blood named Andrew Montour—son of the famous interpreter, Madam Montour—arrived in war paint with a party of his warriors. They talked. Montour convinced Harris to return to his ferry, hike back on the western trail to Herndon. Don't trespass on the eastern shore."

"Convinced by threat or by reason?" asks Alexander.

Tennent chortled. "History remains clouded here."

"Did he return?"

"You tell a man to turn tail and what will he do? Obstinate men rarely have ears to listen. Harris ignored Montour and crossed the Susquehanna instead of heading south. No Indian half-breed was going to tell him what to do. Montour had warned him not to, probably because tensions were high on the Lenape side of the river. Yes, tempers flared and Harris' expedition, as Montour warned, got ambushed right near Penn's Creek. There was a fight. Harris' men scattered. There was killing. Some of Harris' men drowned trying escape over to safety. This Susquehanna—her currents can be very deceptive." Tennent sighed and offered a light, self-deprecating chuckle. "Please forgive an old man for rambling on. What we can't do much with our legs anymore, we make up for with our mouths."

"Some grow their crops with water, some with blood," offered the Colonel. "Appreciate, my boys, what my old friend is telling you. Rarely do we get the chance to hear the real story."

"We misuse the word tragedy, when we mean atrocity," said Tennent bluntly. "That's when I came upon the scene."

"But you still haven't yet explained how you were given your Lenape name," pleaded Alexander.

"There are tales yet to be told," smiled Tennent. "I had been working my way down the Great Island path toward where it intersects with the Penn's Creek path. White men can be so noisy. There they were. Evidently, I had arrived shortly after the Harris party had been ambushed. A small group of the survivors huddled near the river. I hid and tracked them. Instinct told me this wasn't going to be good. White men can be loud."

CHAPTER THIRTEEN

1755

"McCormick, you bastard. How many men are with you?"

"Murdoch, you alive?"

"Made it. Here with Hemelwright, Muir, Ross, Gelder.

"I've got Carlson, McConnell, and Owen.

"Weapons? You got dry powder, enough shot?"

"Damn redskins."

"Don't know where Harris is. I think I saw him jump into the river to escape the bastard savages. Still, we got enough. More than enough. There's nine of us."

"Enough of us, Murdoch, to make it back home safe?"

"Hell, no. I want to get even with those murderers. I saw a band of them head up the creek here. Now's not the time, men, to be squeamish. I saw one of them scalp Packard." Murdoch waved his knife, pantomiming a scalping. "I'm not returning to tell his wife what happened until I have five scalps for every one they took from us. You men ready?"

* * *

"A mile upstream, past the marshy ground, I followed as they came across the first burnt cabin from the original massacre. A man's hacked body lay half buried nearby; the soft parts dined on by animals. A half mile away they entered the ruins of another household not far from the mill on the creek. Two bodies lay there. The sight quickened their pace. The man named Carlson, who had gone on ahead, rushed back to the small band."

* * *

"Quiet. Quiet," this Carlson urged. "Damn heathens are two miles upstream. They're resting in a small clearing. Bold as brass, they even started a small fire. Around the bend here you can see the smoke before the wind washes it out above the tree line. Bold as brass, dirty bastards."

"How many?"

"I only saw them through the brush. Maybe twelve, fifteen?"

"Let's go, men. Carlson, give us warning when we should fan out by twos," ordered Murdoch. "I want them captured. I want them alive when we collect their scalps. Check your flints though, and your priming."

"Murdoch," yelled one of the men.

"Quiet, I said!"

"But I found this jug hidden among the ruins over there."

"Pass it around, boys. Never pass up a chance for a little jug courage."

* * *

"As I said, it wasn't going to be good. I never did see the warriors who had attacked them. Didn't expect to. So I sniffed for smoke, and quickly circled around to find this small band of Indians farther upstream the Kaarondinhah. I hid from them too, even though I discovered that this was no band of Lenape braves on the war path. They wouldn't be so foolish as to light a fire. I was cautious, but only apprehensive about the white men. I treaded close enough without them noticing. They were harmless."

Leaning forward from his padded bench, Tennent told the rest of the tale.

* * *

From behind an oak, Tennent could peer into the small clearing where they were resting. All the adults remained quiet, occasionally bending toward an ear to whisper, but infrequent giggles sounded from investigative children. Tennent enjoyed this peaceful scene of the several children, two younger boys, three young women approaching womanhood. The remainder, except one adult male, were elderly men and women. Only a few were Leni Lenape, the others were Susquehannocks. Yes, harmless, Tennent confirmed in his mind. Must be the last remnant of the Susquehannocks, tatters and scraps now of that great nation. My guess, refugees from Shamokin. They've had it, they're defeated, from the fear of being attacked, from the war cries of the shouting young men demanding revenge. They're beaten down, beaten down by frost, drought, hunger, failure. Heading west with all the others. Tennent smoothed cradled his rifle. Sad, just sad.

The violent shout startled him. The nine white men brandishing flintlocks rushed at the Indians, forcing them into a close huddle. The children started whimpering. He watched as the white men drew out their knives. The band huddled closer to each other, defeated.

Tennant had to think fast. He spat in disgust. And they call the Lenape savages? He noticed one of the men clutching a jug. He shook himself into a disheveled frenzy and tousled his hair. He shifted his hunting frock back over his shoulders. Racing into the midst of the clearing, he shouted at the nine men, "Thank God, thank God. I'm safe! I'm safe! I'm among white men again!" He reached for the jug. "After what I've been through, I could use a drink. I haven't been able to stop for a drink since I came through the Nit-a-nees. Please," he implored. The man pulled the jug out of reach.

"Who are you? What do you mean by this?" growled Murdoch.

"Are you in charge? We don't have much time. We don't. God help us!" Tennent clawed at the arm of the man named Murdoch.

"Are you mad? What are you talking about?"

Tennant whirled around frantically, turning toward the huddled band. Discreetly, he winked at one of the young women. "Listen, I don't care what you do here, but all I can tell you is, that murderous swine Shingas himself, with the hugest war party in full paint out of Kithanink I've ever seen, is about a quarter mile behind me and those murderous braves are moving fast."

"Shingas?" Carlson's voice trembled.

"Don't wet your breeches," snarled Murdoch.

"Do what you want, fight if you want to, but I'm getting out of here! All I can tell you is that the last thing I want Shingas to find on me are a bunch of redskin scalps—especially women's and children's." With that, Tennent rushed frantically into the woods. Murdoch was the first to follow him. Then the rest ran, the fellow with the jug dropping it at the edge of the cleaning.

The Susquehannock party remained huddled, confused by the commotion and sudden rush. The only word they heard and understood was Shingas, whose name terrified them as much as the name terrified the band of Harris' men.

Tennent returned into the clearing smoothing his hair and adjusting his clothes, smiling as he spoke in Lenape. "Peace, friends. Don't worry, the white men ran so fast they have already reached the banks of the Susquehanna. I'm your friend. Though you probably should pack up and continue your journey. I'd recommend you head more northerly."

"And Shingas?" asked a girl approaching womanhood. Tennent winked at her again.

"When you wish rabbits to run, show them the lynx," beamed Tennent.

The band relaxed, then heeded his advice and prepared to leave.

The girl approached Tennent. "You tricked them?" She studied his face. "I do remember you. You were kind to my brother and me a few years ago."

"You are growing into a lovely young woman, Giddy One, a bonny lass." Eagerly, Tennent scanned the party. "Your brother? The Noisy One?"

"He is no longer so noisy. He travels ahead of us by a day to mark the way. My brother now is a protector and has begun writing his own story," she said with pride, standing up straighter, her face uplifted.

"I will find him and let him know what happened here, and where he can find you."

"This too is our story now." Her features softened. "We are a people of stories, such as when you told my brother about the water panther, how we must respect nature. I also said to you that you have the eyes of a cat. Our tradition is that the lynx is the keeper of secrets, keen of sight, even seeing through trees and rocks. The lynx can be a villain but only to those who deserve it. The lynx can reveal hidden truths. As a young woman who one day wishes to be honored with a child, I have seen how the lynx treats its young. When the kitten is scared or in trouble, mother doesn't wait for her kitten to come to her. She rushes toward her young and protects her by grabbing her by the fur of her neck. You, my friend, are very much like the lynx."

She turned to see the oldest man in the band approaching Tennent. "Our chief wishes to speak to you," she said.

"I would be honored."

The chief stood in front of him and studied his face. He placed both of his withered hands on Tennent's shoulders. "Why kill an elk of the white backside when you wish to feed only yourself? Why try to stare down the mountain lion? Better to let him go his way and you yours. When the bear wants to eat, the bear gets to eat all she wants while we wait. We have heard what our Giddy One has spoken to you. You came here sounding like our foe, and you frightened us, but you see when to be wise rather than kill. I see you are a man who kills only when he must. We name you Niankwe, The Lynx."

CHAPTER FOURTEEN

1800

"To this day, Daniel, Alexander, I have never been quite certain if I should consider Niankwe as a compliment."

"Niankwe," said Alexander, savoring the language of the Leni Lenape. "I believe this lynx can teach us when it is wiser to avoid letting our pride cause damage and misery."

"There's more to tell, I regret to say. Unfortunately, the damage and misery didn't stop there. My bluff turned into prophecy. Shingas eventually did invade from Kithanink less than a month later, what we now call Kittanning, with a painted war party, into the region near Burnt Cabins. They called that raid the Great Cove massacre. Forty-seven Dunkard settlers were killed or captured, children included. Many settlers already had fled, but too many Dunkards remained, trusting in their faith and their pacifism. When is devotion admirable? When is it foolish? Sheer brutality and cruelty met their innocent trust. Another atrocity. By June of the next year, the overcrowded village of Shamokin was discovered to have been abandoned. The Oneidas, Onondagas, Lenape, and Shawnee who lived there abandoned the dismal place, fearing retribution. Eye for an eye again. Human nature forced their decision. Their fear of reprisal was the last straw in their daily struggle to hunt for squirrel or groundhog—the absence of hawks a telling indictment, only vultures—their daily struggle to survive the illnesses that swept through the village killing dozens, their struggle to survive the droughts that dried up the creeks and ruined their squash, corn, beans."

Tennent drifted into a distant memory. *The real exam, Reverend Burr*, Tennent confided to himself, *is in simply surviving.* Alexander edged closer to listen.

"Those last reluctant few remaining in Shamokin Village became the final refugees walking toward the western sun. Governor Morris, seizing opportunity for control, immediately summoned Colonels Clapham and Burd to begin constructing Fort Augusta and garrison it. The collapse of Shamokin Village became the Provincial Government's opportunity for full control of the territory. Ebb and flow. The Shikellamies exited, we entered. Morris, at the same time, declared war and decreed a bounty on Indian prisoners and scalps. The bounty promised one hundred thirty pieces of eight for every male above the age of twelve. A woman's scalp fetched the price of fifty pieces of eight."

"I have never heard of this," blurted Alexander.

"Most people prefer their history palatable. Do you wish to be further discomfited? Surely you have heard about the Paxton Boys, good Presbyterians all, who slaughtered, some seven years later, Christianized Susquehannocks. Susquehannocks who were trying to live in Conestoga in peace. They were among the last of that great nation, a great people. Two massacres took place, first in the sanctity of their homes. The second happened two weeks later when the survivors were held in protective custody. They weren't protected."

Alexander looked down at his feet.

"Those boys dared to call themselves militia. Ask your father about how militia should act, like real soldiers, not ruffians and rabble. There was no pride in them. Yes, they were boys, they sure weren't men. Jug courage once again.

They were a drunken mob. Lord, do I get angry when mobs, like a rabid dog, feel unleashed."

"Which leads to increased animosity," contributed William Montgomery. "Even in Chester County, some folks lauded the Paxton Boys, others deplored them. I've always hoped that such behavior was an aberration. Yet my Calvinistic upbringing never lets me rest in that illusion. As another Alexander wrote: 'If men were angels, no government would be necessary.'"

"Hamilton," declared Daniel.

"Could be, but I credit my friend Madison with having authored that essay," corrected Colonel Montgomery.

"And the next line is," contributed Tennent, "If angels were to govern men, neither external nor internal controls on government would be necessary.'" Tennent barked a quick laugh. "Finally, I had had a belly full of it all and headed west to clear my head, my gut, maybe to cleanse my conscience. I, too, roved elsewhere. I couldn't escape it though. At Fort Detroit, I ran right into the Pontiac wars. We map-makers kept drawing lines and marching over them." Tennent rolled his glass between his palms. "I tend to find myself distracted by the worst in our species. At Detroit, I told Colonel Bradstreet that he did a terrible thing tearing up Pontiac's peace belt. Terrible. Terrible also, were all those settler's children made captives who cried and beat against the soldiers when being pulled away from the only parents they ever knew—the only parents they really knew, those Ohi-yo, Shawnee, Delaware, Mingo, Wyandot, Seneca, Cayuga parents who had adopted them, raised them, yes, who loved them as their own. Not that what the Indians did a year earlier to the garrison at Sandusky was particularly noble. Too many snakes. Too many snakes."

The two young men looked at each other, confused by Tennent's reference.

Tennent didn't notice them, for his mind was compassing toward a pleasanter memory. "I finally did return to my Susquehanna and trek upstream—this North Branch is far mightier and inviting than the West Branch—and at last I did visit the headwaters, the source, of this Susquehanna. I've seen lakes before but none so clear or beautiful as there. The lake was as smooth as a lady's looking glass. In Oneida they call the lake the Place of the Rock. There's a smooth, rounded boulder right at the headwaters. There with the help of another fellow like me, and his Mohican friend, I learned how to canoe. Not our kind of clumsy dugout canoes, sturdy enough to handle our Susquehanna rocks and shoals and ledges. Theirs was one of those lake canoes made of birch bark and sticks. You find plenty of birch trees the farther north you travel. You'd think those canoes would be too flimsy. They weren't." Tennent relaxed with a sigh. "Those were good months. Plenty of game. No ambuscades. Good company. No settlements on the lake then. I should have stayed. But no, I felt I had to come back downstream and back into the fray." Tennent sucked his teeth. "Proverbs 26:11."

"I'm certain there's settlements there now," suggested Daniel. "I've heard a little about that country from fellow surveyors. Now that there's peace, the whole country is filling up."

"I suppose. We just keep coming. As an act of penance for my sins, I finally left my friends at that lake and returned. My sins? Me wanting to absent myself from the gifts of civilization. My penance? Finally working as guide and translator for a few missionaries, including that Presbyterian missionary, John Elder. New sins to atone for."

"You worked with Elder?" asked the Colonel abruptly. "He and others planted the seeds for several congregations around here: Old Buffalo, Northumberland, Chillesquaque, Warrior's Run.

"Yes, we worked out of Fort Augusta for a time. Elder hinted to others how proud he was that one of the famous Tennent family was working for him. Funny, for I thought I was working off my debt to God. But then Elder came to believe he was God's anointed one. Excuse my blasphemy—Colonel, Daniel, Alexander. I stayed with him longer than I should have, up until he started bragging about his role with the Paxton Boys. He was their pastor at Paxtang. The Fighting Pastor, they called him. Kept a rifle in the pulpit. Fighting for the wrong gospel, I say. I'm fairly certain no one ever alleged my father, Gilbert Tennent, kept a rifle at the ready in his pulpit. He didn't need to. Father's talk of eternal damnation scared more sinners than any flintlock could."

Alexander and Daniel looked at each other again.

"Here was Elder's catechism," said Tennent as he mimicked the motions, "Return ramrods, make ready, present arms, fire! Well, the way I viewed it, Elder never did repent. He was proud of the massacre. That's all I needed to hear about his brand of Christianity. He explained that their butchery was but a 'momentary excitation of spirit.' Jug spirit it was, and worse. Elder actually blamed the government and the Susquehannocks for what his flock choose to do. Enough, enough." Tennent raised his hands in mock surrender. "I try to remember, but it fails me: 'Judge not lest ye be judged.' Elder, too, had too many snakes in his head."

"Pardon, sir, you've made that allusion that before," said Alexander. "We don't understand. Snakes?"

"'Tis an old, old tale. A Seneca chief told it to me."

* * *

Once upon a time, the original five nations of the Iroquois suffered constant war. Mohawk, Seneca, Cayuga, Oneida, and Onondaga. The lakes, which once were clean and crystal, had turned red from the blood of the women and children murdered in their villages along the banks of those long lakes. The cruelest tribe of all were the Onondaga. The war cry of the Onondaga, echoing from hill to valley, struck terror in the hearts of those whose ears heard the war cries approaching. There would be no escape. The Onondoga were feared because their chief, Tadodaho, was the cruelest leader of all. Even his own people cringed when he walked near them. He not only killed his enemies with great pleasure—he ate his enemies. A man eater. He cared nothing of peace. He was a man of torment who delighted in torment. Tadodaho shouted his own war cry whenever he was eager to kill and bring agony to the innocent. He would shout: "Hwe-do-ne-e-e-e-eh–!" meaning "When will this be? It has not come yet!"

The heart of the Great Peacemaker, with a heart vaster than all the forests, grieved at the plight and despair of his people. The Great Peacemaker felt their pain, heard their laments. With his finger he touched their cheeks and tasted their salty tears. Their suffering at the violent hands of Tadodaho grieved the Great Peacemaker. The Great Peacemaker realized his people must be given a new mind. But how?

One day the Great Peacemaker saw a young brave named Hiawatha walking through his village. Hiawatha wasn't the bravest of warriors. Hiawatha wasn't the cleverest of warriors. He was young and untested. The Great Peacemaker smiled when he saw Hiawatha approach the shore of the stream to cup his hand and refresh himself with a cool drink. When Hiawatha knelt and looked into the water, he did not see the reflection of his own face. He saw instead the image of the Great Peacemaker looking back at him. He saw himself having become one with the Great Peacemaker. The quiet voice of his mind told him what he must do. He, Hiawatha, had received the gift of the new mind. He knew he must take the Great Peacemaker in himself to speak to Tadodaho.

Hiawatha, however, chilled at the thought of what he must do, fearing that Tadodaho would torture him and kill him. But the Great Peacemaker inside Hiawatha gave him a new courage along with his new mind. Together they approached Tadodaho. Seeing him, they saw the reason for his torment. Instead of the clean plucked head of a warrior, Tadodaho's head was filled with snakes, venomous snakes.

Hiawatha, pitying him, began singing a song of peace. Tadodaho at first menaced Hiawatha, threating him with a great knife. Hiawatha kept singing. Soon Tadodaho relaxed and rested on the ground, falling asleep. Hiawatha reached out with a comb and began to remove the snakes, these evil serpents that tormented Tadodaho's mind. Tadodaho, cleansed and freed, awoke from his dream and discovered that the Great Peacemaker had given him a new mind, a straight mind, a mind of peace.

* * *

"That, men, is the tale of Hiawatha, a Mohawk name, I was told. Foolish me still believes there is hope for all of us. Our stories give us hope. Can you guess what Hiawatha's name means?"

They shook their heads.

"No? Legend has it that it means He Who Combs." Tennent ran his fingers through his hair. "We all could use a good combing."

Tennent rose and stretched. "Old bones and old muscles, I fear. Forgive me, young men. I've been much too somber. Too many memories. Time for an old man to take a walk." With a soft whistle, Ruth rose slowly. "Come, Ruth, time for a walk."

The Colonel nodded familiarly.

CHAPTER FIFTEEN

1800

Tennent gazed west toward Montgomery's gristmill and sawmill and the verdant mountain sloping toward the river darkening behind them. A gentle breeze cooled him. Twilight was transforming the trees and mills along the Mahoning Creek into silhouettes. Dark shapes were turning darker, the embers of the orange glow of the setting sun fading before a sweep of gray streaks. *Not as if it is the sun that sets. It is we who move. A matter of perspective, such as when you think you are fixed upon a spot in the river, opposite a certain bend and overhanging limb, only to find the current has drifted you downstream and the landmark is now behind you and the shoreline looks completely different.*

This is contentment. Father did name me his magpie son. Tonight, I sleep here among friends without worries, without being forced to be watchful. Tonight, safe. Contented. He remembered praying with his mother when she'd kiss him goodnight: *Now I lay me down to sleep, I pray thee Lord my Soul to keep, If I should die before I wake, I pray thee Lord my Soul to take. Mother prayed this with me the night before she got sick and died.*

Tennent tugged on the latch to Montgomery's stone house to open the door. He looked back south toward the rise. The river flowed just beyond. Well, some men cherish their ponds. Give me a river. Rifts and rapids, eddies and rocks, freshets and low water. The heavy front door creaked open. Tennent stomped his feet on the top flat-stone step and looked again west toward the gentle valley where the sun settled. Shooing Ruth inside, he followed her into the sitting room.

"That's better. For both of us," announced Tennent to the seated Colonel, whose eyes were half closed. "We needed the walk, and I definitely needed the privy." Tennent breathed deeply. "I cannot believe we've idled away this day. What's become of Daniel and Alexander?"

"Alexander went upstairs to his room," mumbled a dozy Colonel. "He said he needed to write a few thoughts down. A dreamer, that one. You seem to have made a strong impression on him. Travel and adventure are all that boy ever talks about. Well, we'll see how far he roams. Daniel? Daniel has gone home to tuck his daughters into bed and say their prayers together. The whole family will visit tomorrow. He's a good father, a good man. What else could a father hope for?"

"He seems a good man. Both seem to be men of character and steady caliber."

"They are exactly the kind of men this infant nation needs at this hour. Honest men. Our nation is such a babe in the woods. You and I both know that the freedom we won in the Revolution isn't enough. What is required is a moral core. Men of character, honor. You can read your Donne. I prefer my Adam Smith." Montgomery pointed at the books on the table by the window. "For as Smith wrote, we rely upon 'mutual sympathies of sentiments.'"

"Trust me, Colonel, I fully agree. We get it backwards too often. We twist it all up. Prosperity doesn't make you generous. Generosity is prosperity. You, Colonel, are a wealthy man—now don't you try to deny it. Few men are so wealthy. Wealthy in a variety of ways. Fortunately, unlike too many men of your breeding, you value asking yourself, how does wealth benefit if it is held by an immoral man?"

"Exactly the essence of Smith's economics," hastened the Colonel. "It is more than self-reliance. It is the gift of responsibility. We want morality, but rarely can we depend on it. My self-interest in becoming wealthy, as you say, is met when you also are well off, not by me exploiting you. The British with their vice and avarice taught us that lesson. Mayhap that is why our Presbyterian faith argues that the highest calling a man can receive from God is to serve the public good as a Magistrate; as a public servant who, when responsible, we reward. When not, we restrain. Yes, old friend, it does a father proud to see that his life's work will not only carry on but improve with the next generation. I am a fortunate man."

"What about the rest of your children? Tell me before we get too melancholy again."

"The boy's eldest brother, William, writes regularly from Tennessee, where he also works as a surveyor. John and his Elizabeth you might see tomorrow. They have been busy, six children so far. Then there's Robert, four years older than Alexander—he's a born tinkerer, he's got his hands into everything around here. Gristmill, sawmill, a farm of his own over by Fishing Creek east of here. And a store. I see him eventually seeking his own fortune west. There's new opportunity there." The Colonel hummed to himself, then reached for the book leaning atop the other books, opened a dog-eared page, and read: "'Now I further saw, that betwixt them and the gate was a river, but there was no bridge to go over: the river was very deep. At the sight, thereof, of this river, the pilgrims were much stunned; but the men that went with them said, 'You must go through, or you cannot come at the gate.'"

Tennent delighted at the reference. "Pilgrim's Progress, my friend, towards the end of Part I, when Christian is close to reaching his destination after all his trials. He and his companion Hopeful must wade through the water to approach the City on the Hill." He then added his quotation from the book, 'Then they both took courage . . .'"

Pausing to collect himself, Montgomery winked boyishly at his friend, and nodded his head toward the decanter.

Tennent raised his hand. "No, thank you, lest I be scolded by the damsels of Palace Beautiful—Piety, Prudence, Charity, and Discretion." Tennent hummed another quiet laugh. "And your damsels?"

"Hannah, God bless, finally found a husband. You'll see her and her John tomorrow also. So far, no children, which disappoints her. At twenty-five, she is getting on. And Margaret, my youngest, you've already met. I am blessed indeed." The Colonel reached over and broke off a piece of straw from the small whiskbroom leaning against the hearth. He lit the straw from the candle on top of the mantel. Cupping the flame, he lit the candle on the lowboy as well as the sconce hanging on the wall above the bench. He tossed the burning straw into the fireplace.

Tennent watched as the straw blackened and curled. In a whiff of smoke, it was gone. He reached down and scratched Ruth behind the ear. "Do you remember where you were," he asked, breaking the silence, "that morning of the solar eclipse?"

"Strange thing to ask. Yes, yes, I do. Why, I cannot say. But I do. I believe that was around Midsummer's Eve, maybe over twenty years ago. Yes, it was 1778, just before the Big Runaway. Maybe a warning? An omen? Alexander wasn't quite nine months old. We tried to watch it but couldn't stare at it at all, it hurt our eyes. The little ones were puzzled that the sun was disappearing. The darkness unnerved them, despite our adult attempts to explain the science to them. They, as children will, came up with their own far more entertaining explanations."

"I remember it well," mused Tennent, "because a week later the demons were again let loose. June 24, 1778. The sun did disappear that day, though the valley was on fire. It was indeed an omen. You mentioned earlier how I first met Daniel at Fort Augusta during this Big Runaway. I remember that occasion too well."

CHAPTER SIXTEEN

1778

Tennent was posted out of Forty Fort and Fort Wintermute, reporting to Colonel Denison, serving alongside several Leni Lenape scouts whom he trusted as friends. Funny, funny, thought a pensive Tennent. Twenty years ago, these Lenape had allied with the French and fought against us Colonialists and the British. Then our allies were the Iroquois. Come the American Revolution, it's the British who are the enemy, the French our allies, where the Iroquois had allied with the British, and although these Lenape tried to remain neutral, half of the clans allied with us Americans. Tick, tock, swings the pendulum. We are peculiar.

The rumors were hardly auspicious. Fact is, the rumors were frightening because they weren't rumors. Other scouts had reported back to command, warning that a combined force of British regulars and Loyalists, led by a horde of Senecas, were massing in the Tioga region. That morning of June 24 saw Tennent sitting cross-legged near the western bank of the Susquehanna with his Lenape scouts, preparing to head upriver toward Tioga, when the hue of the morning light began to turn an odd shade of copper. They each shaded their eyes and tried to look toward the sun. A portion of its corona seemed flattened. Gradually, darkness curved into the body of the sun.

His Lenape friends welcomed the event as a sign portending the passing of the old and the arrival of the new, of a new light to be born. And my people, Tennent lamented, call them ignorant savages. Their natural poetry celebrated the moon mating with the sun and issuing forth a new birth.

"Tennent!"

"Over here, Nathan. What do you need, Colonel Denison?"

"Once again I need to rely upon you and Covenhoven."

Tennent scowled.

"I share your opinion of the man. Anyone who notches his knife handle for each kill . . . well, regardless, he is efficient."

"We see our tasks differently. We haven't gotten along since the Battle of Princetown."

"Nevertheless . . . Covenhoven has ridden hard from the Loyalsock by way of the Sheshequanink Path. What he's shadowed this last week is evidently worse than some of us feared." Colonel Denison glanced over at Colonel Butler's headquarters in Forty Fort.

"I need both of you men ready and alert," said Denison.

"The British hold Fort Wintermute and Fort Jenkins?" asked Tennent flatly.

"We had hoped for reinforcements from Lower Fort Jenkins and Fort Augusta. There's been no word. We've rejected the British demand for surrender. Between us, the fools are planning to march out and attack. They think swagger and flag, fife and drum can replace discipline. Overconfidence is a guarantee for ruin. Foolish militia! We gave the British Wintermute and Jenkins. We can hold Forty Fort if we don't march out."

"'Let the heathen be wakened," quoted Tennent, "and come up to the valley of Jehoshaphat: for there will I sit to judge all the heathen round about. Put ye in the sickle, for the harvest is ripe: come, get you down; for the press is full, the fats overflow; for their wickedness is great. Multitudes,

multitudes in the valley of decision: for the day of the Lord is near in the valley of decision.'" Tennent looked grim. "The Book of Joel, sir."

"Thank you, Reverend Tennent. May I continue? You and your scouts keep to our flanks. Listen, listen. Be ready to withdraw. Should we collapse, I need Covenhoven and you to warn the settlements—Covenhoven toward the upper West Branch and you, Tennent, downstream all the way to Fort Augusta. Alert any settlers you see. Where there's water, there's settlers."

"I know the country. I've traveled it before."

"Good, good. Good man. There's Lieutenant Van Campen, Moses Van Campen, down by what he calls Fishing Creek. That would be the largest of the tributaries you cross. Most creeks and streams this July you can leap across or are ankle deep. Then there's Fort Bosley where a creek flows into the Chililsaugi. A mill. I hope it's been stockaded by now. Augusta, that's key. If we fall, there is no army between the enemy and those hapless settlements. I've already given orders for riders to head out and give the same warning in the other directions. East to Fort Decker and Fort Penn. South to Northampton County and the Lehigh Valley. Covenhoven has his horse. You want a horse, Tennent?"

"Thank you, but no. I'll be faster running."

"You know the region best."

"You think it likely?"

Denison turned aside and did not answer.

* * *

The battle began with a feint of a British retreat, enticing the militia to pursue. Several volleys were exchanged.

The Colonial militia advanced. When they saw the smoke rising from the captured Fort Wintermute, they assumed the British were in full retreat. The militia quickened their pursuit, assuming their right flank was merely pestered by withdrawing Senecas. Tennent tried to shout loud enough: "Can't you see, the British rangers are lying down!" At that moment they rose up. The Iroquois on the right raced from the woods and attacked in force, such is the temerity of madness, their war cries panicking the militia farmers. The Continental standards fell, not to rise. While reloading, Tennent spotted a bare-chested brave in full paint, with bangles on his arm and a feather sticking out from his scalp-lock, brandishing a smoothbore flintlock. The brave had separated from the assault and rushed toward him. The brave stopped fifty yards away as Tennent was methodically securing his ramrod. The Seneca aimed and fired. No crack, no discharge. Merely a poof and fizzle. "Always check your flint," Tennent muttered, shaking his head. In one fluid motion, he halfcocked his rifle, full cocked it, aimed, and fired. His flint worked. He reloaded. War cries came from the swamp over on the left, another force of Iroquois striking the bewildered militia. The battle was over in a half an hour. The orgy of torture and scalping continued throughout the night. The bilious British and vile Loyalists withdrew from the field, indifferent.

Tennent didn't wait to see how many survivors escaped into Forty Fort or the Fort at Pittston. He had his orders. He ran toward the Susquehanna and headed south. He assumed that Covenhoven and the other scouts were galloping off to deliver their warnings. Securing his shot bag and powder horn as best he could to prevent too much loose slapping, Tennent paced himself. Six steps walking, six steps a fast trot. Warily, he listened and smelled when he walked. There may be a few outliers, he suspected. But he believed it likelier that the Iroquois would be too preoccupied with plunder. What they valued, according to their habits, were the just rewards of war and a defeated enemy. He had to closet his thoughts, shutting the door on them. He had to put away from thinking about what was taking place in Wyoming Valley. He had to shut away his fears for Denison, for the overconfident settlers who now would be fleeing for their lives. Or screaming. His task lay forward, in protecting those downstream, those who could still be saved.

Six steps walking, six steps trotting, working his way through the dense wilderness lining the Susquehanna. Here the trees ruled, making it easier for him to travel the forest floor. Closer to the bank and the underbrush, the brambles, the bracken, and the scrub thicken. The shade gave some relief from the humidity and heat of a Pennsylvania July. He wouldn't have minded a light rain either. The gods were not that kindly disposed. When night deepened, it grew cooler. Time to rest. Looking for a smooth beech, he sat down against it, and listened carefully, grateful for the familiar sounds of the forest. Fatigued, rueful, brooding, he closed his eyes.

Before dawn he woke to resume his mission. First, he checked his flint, opened the frizzen and thumbed out yesterday's priming, his thumbnail long stained from the grains, replacing the priming from the small powder horn that hung from his sash. Then it was run when you can as the crow flies, oft-times veering away from the winding, crooked Susquehanna. Breathe easy, breathe easy. You've got time. From here to Fort Augusta is likely a little farther than Harris' Ferry to Augusta. No cramps please. No pains in the side, either. How do you convey dreadful news to the unsuspecting? Calmly. Factually. Unlike Philippides, I'm not running from Marathon telling the Athenians about victory, nor do I intend to die after I deliver my message. How many creeks so far? Ten, eleven? About an equal number of cabins. Wild orange daylilies bloomed along every bank of every creek. When he noticed signs of habitation, he shouted a halloo to announce himself. Those scattered settlers, when informed of the events, nodded with the stoicism he expected. Some began to look around at what they could pack up, a few simply resumed their chores.

By late afternoon the next day, at what he supposed was the mouth of Fishing Creek opposite the pure water Catawese, he tracked it upstream for less than a league until he came to a clearing in which sat a stockade fort. A young man of light build with a drawn face approached him, carrying an axe. "Welcome to Fort Wheeler," the young man said in greeting. "You don't look as if you are lost. You look like a man with a purpose."

Tennent replied, "I'm a man who could use a rest, a meal, and if I didn't have more miles to go, a hefty tankard of rum."

"We gladly could give you all three—you know your business best."

"What I mostly need is to talk with a Lieutenant Van Campen. Moses Van Campen. I carry news from Colonel Denison and Forty Fort."

"Come inside and sit. Inside there's a gourd you can use and a fresh bucket of spring water. I'm Van Campen."

Tennent laughed aloud. "I was expecting an older man."

"I get that quite often. Even Moses was a baby once. Come."

"The name's Tennent," said Tennent, wiping his sweaty forehead with his neckerchief.

Van Campen gazed upwards. "Weather's close, isn't it? Gray skies aside. July in Penns-woods, eh?"

After Tennent gave his report to Van Campen, along with the three men who gathered around him to listen, Van Campen updated Tennent. "Them heathens have been busy here too, though it grieves me that the Senecas have decided to dance with the devil—a few Seneca are dear friends. Spent the last several weeks being pestered by these devils here about. A small number, but in full paint. Tried to force us to surrender Fort Wheeler here. They didn't. A few of them we sent to their Indian perdition."

"I'm off to Fort Bosley, then Fort Augusta."

"Listen to me, scout, rest here tonight. Lodge here tonight. Get a decent meal. It's about twenty miles yet to travel until Fort Augusta." He signaled to one of the three men. "Tom, we got a few hours of light left. Why don't you go farther upstream and inform our neighbors there's mischief afoot. Have them do the same and spread the word. Them that want to fight can come here awhile or head to Augusta. We ought stand together."

The man named Tom waved in acknowledgement, grabbed his rifle and kit, and left.

"Fort Bosley will take you out of your way about ten miles, though we know a quicker way, then there's Montgomery's Landing at the Mahoning."

"Mahoning, you say? I passed through there several times since the fifties. Nice piece of ground. I figured it would attract settlers."

"The fellow you want to talk with there is a Colonel Montgomery. He moved up here a little over a year ago."

"Colonel William Montgomery?" Tennent repeated.

"You're familiar with him?" asked Van Campen.

"If it's the same Montgomery. We met during the siege of Boston."

"Well, rest now, friend. "I'll wake you before dawn and send you on your way."

* * *

The hike to Fort Bosley at the Chililsaugi did take less than ten miles. Van Campen told him how to track upstream along Fishing Creek, find the second creek that flows into it from the west, follow its to its source, then cut through the pass, descend northwest till you come to the next creek. Follow that to the Chililsaugi. Fort Bosley was, as Denison described, a stockaded blockhouse and gristmill, garrisoned by a handful of men. Arriving there, the news was shared. The men discussed who would run out to inform the Forts located adjacent the West Branch of the Susquehanna.

The steep hill between Fort Bosley and Montgomery's Landing wearied Tennent until he started descending. He stopped at the crest of the hill to admire the cut which led directly to the Susquehanna. The panorama was one of rich verdant growth, wild flowers aplenty. Tennent recognized where he was. The view below refreshed him. Descending into this valley he felt as he had emerged from a cramped cave into fresh air and sunlight. Before him, two mountain ranges stretched to the horizons west and east. The tree-filled mountains sloped gently toward each other, converging into this protected valley. The more he walked into the valley, the more the blue sky opened to him.

The valley and blue sky reminded him of one afternoon along the wide Hudson in Newark when he and a young lady enjoyed what they called back then a French *pique-nique*. He lay down on the blanket. She reclined on the blanket also, stretching out in the opposite direction. Their faces were merely inches from each other, her forehead to his chin, his chin to her forehead. They inhaled each other's breath. They were too happy to cheapen the moment by talking.

After walking a league into the valley, he came to a trickling creek where, he remembered, over twenty years ago he had fished for brown trout. Tennent removed his hat and wiped his brow, running his hand through his hair. He soaked his neckerchief and wrapped it around his neck. Despite it being July, the creek, shaded by columns of hemlocks, flowed steadily. I do remember this place, Tennent reflected silently. This is the Mahoning. Mahonhanne in Leni Lenape, the name for a stream flowing from a salt lick. A good place to hunt. A good place.

Farther on, two furlongs before the Mahoning meandered into the Susquehanna, Tennent spotted, toward his left, a log cabin built on a slight rise. Behind the cabin, a small pen of robustious and noisy shoats rooted through the mud, shoving each other. Beside the pen stood an open shed in which a cow was hitched, methodically chewing hay from a basket attached to the wall, her calf reaching under momma to nurse. Several other cabins were tucked about the cultivated fields. The cabins reminded Tennent of eggs in a comfortable and warm nest. A twinge of envy at the prospect of such a life surprised him.

A man in a brown waistcoat, his sleeves rolled up above his elbow, his dark hair tied back, came around the corner of the cabin into the front yard carrying a hoe. Several chickens scrambled after him, competing for bugs in the grass. Tennent starting walking toward the man across a field cluttered with stumps.

The man in the field spotted the stranger approaching him. That he wore buckskin and fringed leggings, hunting shirt and a floppy hat, didn't alarm him. Neither did the fact that the man cradled his Lancaster rifle in the hollow of his arm, or that he also was armed with a large knife in the sheath sewn onto his right legging, with two Indian tomahawks tucked into his wide belt.

"Welcome, stranger," said the man amiably.

"Stranger, indeed. How about old friend? Or has the sedentary life of a farmer softened your brain, Colonel?"

"Huh?" wondered the man. "Tennent? Really? Is it you? It is you!" he exclaimed. "How? Why? I'm all at sea here." The hoe fell to the ground.

They shook hands warmly, grasping each other's elbows with their left hands.

"Please, Tennent, come in, come in," the Colonel invited effusively.

"We'll have that chance soon, I promise."

"What brings you here?" The man stepped back and examined Tennent. "Knowing you, I doubt it's pleasure."

"I wish it were." Tennent proceeded to describe the events of the last four days.

"I see," said the Colonel, unfolding his sleeves.

"Will you take charge here and see that the word gets delivered? I trust each man has enough powder and shot. We need Colonel Montgomery back in uniform, sir." Tennent's speech turned clipped. "Bosley said they would send word to the West Branch forts. Swartz, Freeland, Boone's on Muddy Run. A rider should already have reached the Lawi-saquick and Legauihanne. Sorry, I mean the Loyalsock and the Lycoming."

"I wish I could offer you something."

"You will. We'll save it for happier days. When we have something to toast. I must run to Fort Augusta now and alert the garrison. Who is in command there now, do you know? Is it still Sam Hunter?"

"I believe so. I haven't had a chance yet to introduce myself to him. We only came here a year ago."

"Colonel, now's your chance to meet him. I know you're going to do what you feel you must do according to your sense of duty, but I do hope the women and children will be escorted to the safety of Augusta."

"I get your drift. You've never been one to panic. How soon do we have?"

"I doubt any of the enemy were on my heels," he rejoined. "The British sure weren't. Maybe a few small raiding parties of braves. I'm no tactician. I cannot, however, see the British foolish enough to split up their forces. If that is the case and they remain in force, they have four choices: march east toward the Delaware river, or south to the Lehigh, or west to the upper West Branch where they can possibly meet up with Iroquois coming down through elk country, or, last, they come downstream toward us here and take on Fort Augusta. Your guess, Colonel. I'm just a lowly scout."

"Just so long as your marksmanship is still what it used to be."

After intense days of urgency and danger, he couldn't resist. "Ach, my honor'd neebor," Tennent inflected with a devious grin as he nodded his head over his left shoulder. "Ae, I'm weel s'posing my shot could find a spot on one of beasties ye call buffalo sae I hear'd tell of wanderin' 'bout over yonder westerly." He patted the stock of his Lancaster rifle, wiped the brass patch lid, and sighed with a smile. "I've carried this admirable flintlock ever since I had it made by John Baker in Lancaster back in '48. She's been a good piece. But sadly, Colonel, she's had too much opportunity, and, as a result, my aim has had more than its share of practice. Well, you take care. I must be off. I'm thinking it might be quicker to stay on the north side of the Susquehanna."

"It would be. There's a semblance of a road between here and the confluence now."

"See you at the Fort."

CHAPTER SEVENTEEN

1778

Fort Augusta looked the brute she was intended to be. She didn't compare with the eastern fortifications, such as star-shaped Ticonderoga, which protected the upper Hudson River Valley; or Philadelphia's Mud Island Fort, guarding the Delaware and Schuylkill Rivers. But unlike both of those forts, Augusta, controlling the confluence on the Susquehanna's West Branch and North Branch along with all the various Indian trails that ranged out like spokes from the former Shamokin Village, still remained in American hands. She was commissioned originally by the British for securing the frontier during the French and Indian War. Minor skirmishes ranged around the fort, like crows fluttering into the stalks to steal kernels of corn. Never was Augusta seriously threatened with assault or siege, her very location deterring the enemy. She was formidable, principally because she was remote; and because the Delaware, Shawnee, and the Iroquois preferred ambush combat. In a region where most forts were improvised from stone houses or gristmills, Augusta was a brute, especially when all that the enemy could muster would be small arms.

She was small, two hundred square feet, only one-third the effective range of a long rifle. Tennent's rifle could kill at two hundred yards. Log walls—vertical facing the river, horizontal like a cabin to the rear —framed the fort itself which contained the barracks, the colonel's and officer's quarters, and the powder magazine, along with the ever-essential well. Bastions and parapets had been constructed at each of the four corners, equipped with cannon. These triangular bastions were designed to insure killing fields around the entire Fort. The log walls were fronted by sharp abatis should attackers breach the surrounding palisade and still survive to cross the ditch.

After the exhausted conclusion of the French and Indian War, and before the formal 1763 Treaty of Paris officially ended that war, Augusta had served principally as a major trading post, offering respite and security from ambush for weary settlers and missionaries. Revolution drafted her back into military service.

Tennent stood alongside Colonel Hunter when the first of the refugees started to arrive. A few rafted with their belongings down from the nearer settlements of the West Branch. Many of those who hiked down the Catawissa Trail carted their belongings in barrows. Those who crossed over from Northumberland had to abandon their carts before boarding raft or dugout so they could be shuttled to Shamokin Island, which they crossed on foot, to again be ferried to the drawbridge of Fort Augusta. The livestock that some farmers wanted to save were herded into the open area between fort and stockade. Hunter's adjutant, with the aid of the quartermaster, registered the evacuees as they arrived and assigned them to their temporary quarters. The adjutant was particularly interested in finding out from those who arrived at Fort Augusta the names of those who chose to remain behind, so he could keep an accurate accounting should the worst take place. The farmers, each shouldering their rifles, gathered silently inside the front gate near the well while the women and children congregated outside their assigned barrack toward the rear of the fort. The women brightened when they saw the faces of friends and neighbors and began chatting as if this were a church meeting. They admired the newest babies, complimented each other on their shawls and caps. The women were as resolute as their men. None wept nor dared display any signs of alarm. The children, excited by the adventure, chased each other round, frolicking with the soldiers who garrisoned Augusta. A few of the boys ventured to the northeast bastion and took turns sitting on the cannon and pretended to fire it into a horde of imaginary Indians.

The Montgomery family arrived; the Colonel's wife holding her baby, her other hand holding the hand of a shy little girl. A young man tried to corral a rambunctious toddler from rushing off to join the other boys. Following them was a delicate looking woman pulling against the tugging hand of a young boy. William Montgomery led his brood directly toward Tennent and Colonel Hunter.

Tennent introduced Montgomery to Hunter. Said Hunter, tapping the hilt of his sword, "Powerfully glad to meet you, sir. Tennent here acquainted me with the situation and your particular history. He speaks well of you."

"As I do of him."

Hunter stepped back to study Montgomery. Montgomery no longer looked the farmer. In deference to Hunter, he had decided not to wear his uniform; although, like Tennent, he was armed for a fight. He cradled his long rifle; his powder horn and small horn for priming the pan were slung across his body; his gun pouch slung over the opposite shoulder. His deerskin shot bag hung on his hip; the touch hole wire hanging from his sash; his knife and hatchet tucked into his belt. His tricorn hat was set square on his head.

"Colonel Hunter, if you'll let me get my family situated, we can talk, and then we can confer with the local men over at the well. I assure you, they already know the situation. My own two older boys, William and John, have remained behind with their Uncle Daniel to keep an eye out."

"Of course, Colonel." Hunter pivoted. "Tennent, when you have time, I have duties for you." Hunter looked up at the sky, the sun drifting behind the hills on the south side of the Susquehanna. "Full moon in a day or two. Safer when you can see."

Tennent clucked his tongue and quoted from the Book of Isaiah: "Also I heard the voice of the Lord, saying, 'Whom shall I send, and who will go for us?' Then said, 'Here am I; send me.'"

Hunter shook his head in mock disgust. "I've never met a more blasphemous son of a—" Hunter hesitated, then finished, "—preacher."

"Most of us are, Colonel. Most of us are."

"Come, Tennent," waved Montgomery in a familiar and jovial manner. "Time to meet my family." Tennent nudged Montgomery and nodded in the direction of the women. One woman appeared anxious, fretful. She shivered. She held a cloth to her face. She seemed close to bawling. Her little boy, sensing his mother's nervousness, stopped tugging to get free and instead huddled close to her.

Montgomery explained, "That's my brother's wife, another Margaret in the family. They lived in Philadelphia."

Tennent understood.

"My wife, Isabella, will console her."

Between spasms, his sister-in-law complained, "I should never have left Philadelphia. We had such a beautiful

home. We didn't have to run from the British occupation."
Isabella, holding her infant, simply listened and rubbed her
nephew's back.

The young man gave up trying to restrain his brother,
walked up and glowered at Tennent, then marched to confront his father with folded arms. "Father," the boy pouted,
"John gets to stay and fight. Why can't I? I shoot better
than he can."

"Daniel," said a stern Montgomery, "you do what you
are told. He's older than you by a year, and your job is
to protect your mother and your brothers and sister. She
needs you here with her, as does your aunt." Montgomery
remained firm. "You do what I say, son. We don't know
how long this will last."

Tennent asked Montgomery for permission to speak
to Daniel. He knelt down in front of the boy. "Alright,
Indian fighter." Daniel's eyes widened. "First of all, a good
woodsman listens to his father. Second, a scout does his
duty as he's ordered. Understood?" Tennent peered up at
Montgomery. "Tell you what. Every scout needs a real
tomahawk. Since you're going to protect the folks here, if
your father gives his permission, you take this." He pulled
his tomahawk from his belt and, when Montgomery nodded, handed it to Daniel who held it up greedily.

"You should know, Daniel, that this tomahawk was a
gift to me from one of Shikellamy's own sons. Shikellamy
was the Oneida chief who used to live right here. See that
hill over there, Blue Hill? That's the profile of his face up
there in the mountainside." Tennent turned aside to look
up again at the Colonel and winked. "The story goes that
after Shikellamy died, Shukwaya'tisu, the Great Spirit, sent

a dozen of his bravest warriors from the sky and they carved the rock face one night so that we might remember him as a great chief who always wanted peace between his people and ours."

* * *

The British didn't divide their forces. They also opted to ignore Fort Augusta. The settlements along the upper West Branch were far more unfortunate. The refugees of Augusta could see at nighttime the far distant glow of burning homes and forts.

"Snakes," muttered Tennent. "A headful of snakes."

After Tennent and other scouts reconnoitered along both branches of the river and declared them safe, most of the families who had evacuated to Augusta eventually returned to their farms.

* * *

Next July, late July, bloodshed came home.

Tennent arrived at Fort Freeland only to find a burnt log house, a smoldering stockade, and embers of an outbuilding. Reaching down, he picked up a caltrop. "This is an act of desperation," he spoke to himself. "These iron crow's feet are fine if you're fighting cavalry, unlikely that an Indian is going to be foolish enough to step on it."

He had been pursuing a war party of British soldiers and Iroquois, who may have been a feint to draw General Sullivan and his forces out of the Wyoming Valley. Feint or not, figured Tennent, it was reprisal for the Continental Army daring to strike back. From their paint, they were Senecas. His hope was to find opportunity to skirt the force and alert the men at Bosley, Boone's, and Freeland. He had lingered too long at Fort Bosley, where a runner reported about the ambush at Freeland that had taken place a week before, Indians killing some of the men who were working the fields surrounding Freeland. Nobody knew if they were part of the larger force or an independent raiding party. Tennent shook his head. *I should have gone directly to Freeland. I should have.*

The site and smell of the ambush was hard to miss. The drone of furious insects. The cacophony of crazed, glutted crows. The familiar stench of men become carrion, bloating in the humidity. He tightened his neckerchief around his mouth. From where Fort Freeland once stood, he followed the creek a short distance downstream. Thirteen mutilated bodies he counted, each scalped. The signs indicated that those who weren't dead before they were scalped were tortured—ears, fingers, noses lay strewn about, eyes punctured. Tennent circled around, studying the tracks, picturing what the tracks instructed. "Damn snakes," Tennent swore. "Damn the British who stood here and just watched."

Later, an old farmer, one of the group of survivors who made it to safety at Fort Augusta, told Hunter how the twenty-one men defending Freeland were persuaded to surrender. Listening at his desk, Hunter rested his elbows on the desktop and rubbed his temples. The British commander, the old farmer described, ordered the women, children, and old men to evacuate immediately, forcing them to walk the harsh miles to Fort Augusta. The fate of the men remained uncertain. Another survivor, a man who had been stationed at Fort Boone, reported how they feared it was half the garrison from Fort Boone who had been massacred along Warrior Run. Hearing from a runner about Freeland's plight, Captain Boone had rushed with volunteers to assist the defenders of Freeland. They likely would have crossed Warrior Run at that spot. They must have underestimated the number of the enemy they were facing, the man suggested.

"Evidently," replied Hunter.

CHAPTER EIGHTEEN

1800

"I often wish," Tennent said softly to the Colonel, "I could rinse my brain of all my bad memories, banish all my regrets, all the unkind words spoken, all the harm I have caused those innocents who got in the way. If only I could wash away all the blood."

The Colonel tried to protest Tennent's confession.

Tennent raised his palm at the Colonel. "Then I realize my folly. As if I could cleanse my memories. Memories are like tributaries. Water will flow where water will. What's upstream invariably flows downstream. God bless, rather, my disquietude. To erase our bad memories erases who we have become today. The fortunate among us admit them, learn from them, making ourselves more human than inhuman, remembering to name them instead of letting them name you. Still, the ghosts of those I failed haunt me still."

The Colonel folded his hands together.

"Have we been decent men?" wondered Tennent, his penetrating eyes staring outside into the night sky through the western window, which offered a reflection of the burning candles from the table and sconce. "What will they say about us? What kind of eulogy?"

"That'll be for them to write," mused Colonel Montgomery. "Although, old friend—or should I say, Niankwe—I'd rather they simply tell the story rather than judge us." Montgomery drained the decanter into their glasses. The candle on the mantel flickered.

"*Slàinte mhath*," Tennent toasted. They lifted their glasses, clinked them, and drank the last of the rye.

Said Tennent, wiping a few tears with the back of his hand, "I was thinking about tomorrow. I look forward to meeting the rest of the family later in the day, but if I remember rightly, there's that Beaver Dam above your Roaring Creek on the other side of the Susquehanna. Roaring Creek? I visited there years ago. Roaring? More like a pleasant purr. I hear that's the name for it now instead of Popemetang. Popemetang in Lenape. The creek of rapids and small waterfalls. Still, it promises some good trapping if I get up before sunrise."

Montgomery began to reach into his ruby red waistcoat pocket. "Let me give you a few coins for the Gearhart Ferry. Despite the flood back in March, the water is low this summer. Still, Gearhart knows his pools and rocks. He marks the water level by that large, oblong boulder with strange pockmarks almost halfway across."

"Thanks, I appreciate it, but no. Ruth will enjoy wading through the river. Ruth's mostly Spaniel. What plans for tomorrow? Yes, I expect I'll cross over."

About the Author

The spirit of the Leatherstocking Tales has come to the Susquehanna Valley through the pen of **Robert John Andrews** in his novella, *A Susquehanna Tale*. Stories communicate best the layers of truth. Retired from serving for nearly thirty years as pastor of the Grove Presbyterian Church, Danville, Pennsylvania, after having first served for eleven years as pastor of the Penningtonville Presbyterian Church, Atglen, Pennsylvania, Andrews remains a popular local newspaper columnist, community and church leader, and public speaker on religious and historical topics. His first foray into publishing was his Civil War historical fiction, *Nathaniel's Call*, which won the Presbyterian Writer's Guild First Book Award, the first Print-On-Demand so awarded. Danville remains his home. From this river community he has learnt to cherish this region's rich history and to love the tale of its river.

LOVE IN THE DARK

Barbara Cartland

Barbara Cartland Ebooks Ltd

This edition © 2018

ISBNs

9781788670890   EPUB

9781788670906   PAPERBACK

Book design by M-Y Books
m-ybooks.co.uk